The Secret of Closings

Laura Walker

Published by Laura Walker, 2023.

This is a work of fiction. Similarities to real people, places, or events are entirely coincidental.

THE SECRET OF CLOSINGS

First edition. March 7, 2023.

ISBN: 979-8215059982

Written by Laura Walker.

Table of Contents

To anyone who has ever aspired to live in a castle

CHAPTER ONE

Parsons Running, April 1802

The fire ravaged the ballroom. The castle was going up in flames and not a thing could be done to stop it. All the servants could do was stand and stare in stunned silence as the yellow glare of the escalating flames lit up their faces. The flames continued raging until the fire was contained, leaving the entire western wing engulfed with the smoke billowing out. The ballroom remained a saturated, ebony shell with woodwork all brittle and flaked. Family secrets and memories were buried along with it. A heritage was destroyed forever.

Bodies were taken out on stretchers. Footsteps of a forlorn lady echoed throughout the hall. Her loud sobs reverberated down the stairs. A figure dressed in black sat on the floor, her body rocking from side to side as she cradled her face in her hands.

Silence, eerie silence followed as the desolation set in.

Then the blackness came along with the thick, dense fog of nightfall and the castle loomed Gothic in its stillness.

As the years passed, the estate became rough and overgrown, returning to a chaotic, natural state. The wind gently swayed the tall grasses in abandoned gardens. Wild bushes made a claim on every vestige of land left over to them. Parsons Running, once a pleasant, quiet village, home to friendly people, was now a mere distant memory of better times.

The mist hung over them too.

STANTON MOORE, JANUARY 1832

The misty rain had set in. Relentlessly, it beat down on the windows at Buckley House and on its vast walls with imposing pillars of bone white. The estate was tranquil with a serenity of vast proportions. The house was situated within park-like grounds, below a deep ravine, and sat on the outskirts of the country village of Stanton Moore. Like every village it had its highs and lows.

On the fourth floor, Miss Scarlett Henson had shifted her position to the window seat of her dressing room an hour ago. Restlessly watching the rain, she perused a letter from her best friend Miss Catherine Kettering, who happened to be staying in London for the week to visit her Aunt Sylvie. She gave an endless description of her extensive property.

'I am longing to come home and see you again, my dear Scarlett. I have no one with whom to share my secrets. Nor have someone to speak sense back to me. I fear I shall go mad before the week is through. Furthermore, I miss the country air, for London is so huge and noisy in comparison.'

"Dear Catherine," Scarlett murmured with a sigh.

The girls, who had recently turned one and twenty, had grown up in Stanton Moore. They had rarely been in town, let alone to London, nor had they yet attended a public ball. This was about to change when they attended Lord and Lady Simm's large estate on the outskirts of London in the autumn. To be guests at the Simm's ball was considered the highest honour there was to be had.

Scarlett completed the reading of her letter and stood up to move about the room. Her muslin, embroidered shawl slid to her waist, exposing slender, ivory shoulders. Curls of golden wheat draped loosely down her back.

She pictured herself dressed in stiff silk with a flowing skirt, shimmering crystal flowers amongst her soft waves. A handsome gentleman kissed the satin gloved hand she held out to him, and he twirled her onto the dance floor.

A light tap at the door roused her from her thoughts of the London ball. Upon her calling out, "Enter!" A petite maid with mousy brown hair promptly entered the room.

"Ah, miss, it isn't the weather to go riding this afternoon," the maid said in her strong, Irish accent.

"No, Naima. I had anticipated as much. You will have to ask Lady Salisbury to cancel our riding session for today," Scarlett said.

"Right you are. I'll just be fixing your hair, then?"

"Yes. Thank you, Naima."

Scarlett settled herself on the chair at her dressing table as Naima got to work dressing her hair.

Naima Patterson arrived from Ireland last year, employed by Mrs Lavinia Henson, Scarlett's mother. Her husband, Mr John Henson, who liked a detailed perusal of the *Stanton Times*, had discovered the following advertisement.

'A young Irish woman with previous experience and excellent references seeks a position as a housemaid in a large household.'

Naima thus came to Buckley House and a week into her position saw her and Scarlett become best friends. No one except Naima was allowed to dress her and see to her hair. She simply couldn't manage without her.

"You'll be thinking of the ball, Miss Scarlett?" Naima asked, looping braids of Scarlett's hair around her ears before gathering it into a topknot.

"That's what I was thinking about when you entered," Scarlett said.

"I thought you would be, miss. They were talking about it downstairs between them," Naima said, glancing through the mirror that highlighted the freckles scattered across her cheeks.

"I'm sure they were. I'm sure they do speak about it often when I'm not present," Scarlett said with a sigh.

"Why are you sighing there? Aren't you looking forward to it?" Naima asked.

"I can't say, Naima. However, I'm sure my mother will want to marry me off to the first rich gentleman that presents himself to me."

"Well... that is unfortunate, but surely you'll be anticipating the dancing now, won't you?"

"I'm sure I am. I do like dancing and music so much."

"There you are, then. You shan't want for partners, Miss Scarlett, if I may say so? As for your former concern, you should take care to fall in love with a rich gentleman now, then there will be no argument."

"If only it was that simple, Naima."

"I know. It will turn out all right in the end, you'll see," Naima said.

Scarlett sighed, twisting a hair grip around in her hand. "I wish I had your confidence."

"Must be the Irish blood in me. Mama was always the positive one," Naima said.

"What's this you are saying? Naima," said the firm voice of the lady of the house.

"Oh," Naima said, spinning on her heel. She swept into a curtsy.

"You may be dismissed now, Naima, Miss Scarlett's hair looks just fine," Mrs Henson said, clapping her hands.

Naima glided from the room. She closed the door gently behind her.

Mrs Henson perched on the bed behind the dressing table.

Scarlett stared expectantly at her mother through the mirror. She was a very attractive woman, and she had proudly passed her good looks onto her daughter. She had the same golden locks of hair and piercing green eyes that shone like emeralds.

"You spend too much time talking to Naima, Scarlett. I don't know what I shall do with you. She is filling your head with all that Irish nonsense. You will never marry well if you pick up on all her vulgarity. I have told you before, servants are not to be conversed with beyond what is necessary," Mrs Henson said, glaring back at her daughter.

"I'm sure I don't know what you mean, Mama," Scarlett replied.

Mrs Henson studied her almond shaped fingernails as she said, "Clearly, you don't. I'm relieved to hear it, for it shows you have not been tainted by her already."

Scarlett kept up a submissive silence, not because she agreed with her mother, but because she had learnt that this was the best course to take when her mother was being righteous.

"What a pity you must cancel with Lady Salisbury today. You need her company as much as possible if you're to become anywhere near the great lady she is. I know what we shall do. I will invite her over for dinner this evening. What do you say to that?" Mrs Henson said.

"Whatever you say, Mama."

"I'll run down and catch Naima before she sends word to Salisbury Manor."

INSTEAD OF RIDING IN the afternoon, Scarlett accompanied her mother on a shopping trip in the village to indulge Mrs Henson's extravagance. The carriage pulled up outside a row of dainty shops with panelled windows and a horizon of smoke from the recently built railway station. Their ears were met by the trains hooting past.

As they alighted, they held the hem of their skirts above the ground to avoid the dust. They paused as a horse drawn carriage clattered in front of their path. Mrs Henson eyed it with a scowl because for her it was an evil machine drowning out an opportunity to converse on her ideal gown. Scarlett, however, found relief in the interruption from what she saw as her mother's constant chatter.

Although Stanton Moore could in no way boast of the retail outlets of London or Bath, both Mrs Henson and Scarlett found a reasonable supply of couture at the boutique. They never had gowns made up anywhere else.

One window they passed was filled with delicious pies and twisted loaves. The homely smell of baked goods took over from the rotting odour that drifted in from the agricultural farms nearby. Scarlett had to restrain herself from dragging her mother inside to sample some fresh produce.

Of course, eating in the street was not ladylike, and her mother would scold her for her lack of propriety, even though Scarlett had seen her mother, on more than one occasion in their kitchen, sneaking a piece of the leftover pie when she thought no one was watching her. But she knew it was best not to disobey her. This memory brought a conversation to mind she'd once overheard between her mother and father when she was just six years old. The maid had put her to bed one night. She was restless and crept downstairs in only a night dress, clutching her teddy bear. The drawing room door had been slightly ajar and twice her father mentioned her mother's peasant upbringing, also how she'd gone up in the world since marrying him. She had known then why her mother wanted to take her place in society. Furthermore, why she considered it imperative Scarlett behaved herself.

They made it to the shop, which was the real reason for their visit, and once inside, Scarlett's fingers tingled. Like an excited youth at her first public gathering, she hurried through the colourful maze of fabrics, running her hand across each luxurious roll. Some were soft and silky, while others were firm and crisp. They reminded her of ladies and gentlemen dancing in circles, which made her head spin.

ON THE WAY HOME, THEIR carriage made an unexpected detour.

It wasn't until they had passed the sign for the next village of Parsons Running that they realised what was happening.

Mrs Henson tapped on the roof with her umbrella. "Aikman, you should have taken a left at the last turn. Go back at once."

A sting of pity arose in Scarlett's heart for the new coachman.

The carriage halted.

"I'll have to find a suitable space. Bear with me," Aikman said.

Mrs Henson slumped in her seat as the carriage moved on. "I knew your father shouldn't have hired him."

Parsons Running was now in sight. Each of the mud houses lining the village had their own apple trees and children gathered the fruit from the ground into weaved baskets.

Scarlett struggled to understand the unease that arose in her breast as the carriage circumnavigated the village. Even though the two villages were affiliated with each other in society and manners, and not much gossip escaped from there that was not first heard in Stanton Moore, there always seemed to be a sense of eerie silence and unease in that part of the county. She had heard talk of the decades-old fire that happened at the castle. Apparently, it had never been lived in since. Although she had never seen Closings Castle or the estate, the thought made her shiver when she imagined the cries of the people ringing out in her mind. She imagined the castles inhabitants were as important as the Salisbury's were to Stanton Moore. She wondered if the village had ever recovered from such a shock.

CHAPTER TWO

Almost as soon as they'd reached the house, Scarlett traversed the passage leading to the library without even stopping to remove her coat.

As she pushed open the sliding aperture of the entrance, an earthy smell like that of a saturated forest floor met her nostrils, reminding her how much she loved old books. She was sure to find amongst them a journal on the history of their county. She had always considered books to be a window to the imagination and she described many of them as heart-warming, insightful, even laugh-out-loud funny. Her mother didn't like her to read too many novels, calling them childish and giddy, but she always allowed her to learn about history and geography from them, aided by her father.

She knew from previous experience of using the library that the collection on heritage was always located on the top shelf. She ascended the step ladder, being welcomed by a portrait of clouds and cherubs, and scanned the titles.

At last, she came to an ancient book, and as she lifted it from the shelf, a stronger musty smell hit her. The pages almost fell apart in her hands when she opened it.

She ran a finger down the contents section. Parsons Running was listed in the middle of the book. She turned to the appropriate page. Closings was pictured after the fire, but the picture was too old and dark to see it in all its glory.

She held the page up to the light, just making out a burnt-out shell piercing right the way through the centre of the castle. That it was once grand, she had no doubt. She would have loved to have seen it as it once was.

During history lessons she'd often read about ancient castles, becoming intrigued by them. As theatres of history, they set the stage for many conflicts. They were the structures of the Medieval age, and she had a good deal of fond memories of visiting the fairy tale chateaus of France as well as an Austrian schloss in the Alps.

She turned her attention to some writing beneath the picture.

'Closings Castle was home to the Lattimer family for many generations. Tragically, the infamous fire of 1802 took the lives of Mr and Mrs Lattimer, as well as two servants, but their young son Frank survived. He lives to inherit the property when he is of age.'

Scarlett paused.

Frank Lattimer must be of age. Why doesn't he return to claim what's his?

'When, or if the current master of the castle will return, is unclear, but a great chasm will need to be overcome to maintain the standing the household held previously in the county.'

It could be that the chasm is too wide for him to undertake. What a pity.

After leafing through the remaining pages, she found there was no further mention of the castle after this. She closed the book with a thud and returned it to the shelf.

After handling the book her fingers felt damp, picking up the same hue of the pages. What would Lady Salisbury say if she went to dinner smelling like this?

She descended to the safety of solid ground, running to the bathroom to scrub them.

LORD AND LADY SALISBURY lived about two miles away from Buckley House. Although it was not as grand as Closings Castle, Salisbury Manor was considered one of the finest houses in all of Stanton Moore. It had lost some of its sparkle with ivy creeping up the windows, but these features added to the influence of families like theirs. The mazed courtyard had always been exquisite and mesmerising.

The Salisbury's were late arriving at Buckley House, as was to be expected of society people.

The Henso"s awaited their arrival in the drawing room. Mr Henson faced the window, a glass in one hand. All you could see of him from behind, where his wife and daughter were sitting beside each other, were his grey, balding head and large bulky shoulders. He looked much like a badger dressed in a dinner jacket.

"Seems a shame to bring the Salisbury's out," he said, pulling a face at the rain battering on the glass.

Mrs Henson scowled. "Nonsense, John."

Lavinia Henson wore a gown with humongous stripes. She paraded the skirt along the sofa with the sharp pleats mirroring folds of paper. A point de gauze around her shoulders satisfied her love of lace. Scarlett compared this with her ankle-length pleated dress that she preferred even though the gigot puffy sleeves made her naturally slender arms appear blown up like a balloon. The low band around her middle made up for this effect as it offset her tiny waist and she didn't look too wide.

"Only. . ." John started.

"Don't say it," Lavinia scolded.

"I'm in the throes of my global travels in the office...!"

Lavinia threw up her hands. "Not that blasted globe. I would never have bought it for you if I'd known...!"

"Where did you get to?" Scarlett asked, prompting a frown from Lavinia.

John spun to face his daughter, revealing walnut brown angular whiskers, narrow at the top, and a large square head that looked too heavy for his shrunken shoulders. "America. I discovered a whole new society..."

Harper, the family butler, announced Lord and Lady Salisbury in his usual professional manner, which manifested itself as a quiet cough behind his hand. His tall, lank figure towered in the doorway.

Lady Salisbury pushed past the butler to hurry him on, the bell-shaped hem of her dress swishing. The feathers protruding from her mauve tinged crown reached the ceiling. She was closely followed by her lord. Lord Salisbury was a serious, quiet man, who wore an eyeglass in his left eye. His other eye blinked furiously beside it. Scarlett had always supposed this was a nervous twitch caused by the persistent threat of getting scolded by his wife.

Mrs Henson smoothed the knots of hair that extended out from the crown of her head.

"Lavinia, what a dreadful day it has been. If there is one thing I cannot stand, it is a servant who fails to do their duty," Lady Salisbury gushed in a shrill, staccato voice.

"Indeed, Lady Salisbury. I'm awfully sorry if we've inconvenienced you this evening," Mrs Henson said, shifting to a standing position. She held out her arms.

They exchanged the usual greetings of hugs and kisses, then made their way to the dining room.

"Don't you worry, Lavinia, for bringing us out this evening. Your daughter needs the company of refined society as much as possible if she is to marry well," Lady Salisbury said as they took their places at the table that filled the length of the room.

"She certainly does, as I'm always telling her myself," Mrs Henson said.

Mrs Henson and Lady Salisbury continued to discuss Scarlett as though she wasn't present at the table.

Her father conversed solely with Lord Salisbury.

"Something must be done about the matter of Garner's cheating at golf. It really must be sorted, Mr Henson," Lord Salisbury said.

The conversation between Mrs Henson and Lady Salisbury, on the other hand, had turned to the usual society gossip.

"Mrs Craven has taken on a new butler as the old one didn't suit, but as I said to her, do any of them? He had become too old and slow, you know? That's servants for you. What a to-do they cause," Lady Salisbury said. She swirled some wine around her mouth like a connoisseur.

The butler and footman shuffled uneasily on their feet at her observation.

"I was telling Scarlett only today how little one should have to do with servants, wasn't I?" Mrs Henson said, awaiting a reply from her daughter.

Scarlett attempted none.

"Oh no. You can never be too careful," Lady Salisbury said.

Mrs Henson leaned across the table. "Why, only this afternoon, Aikman ended up in Parsons Running of all places, instead of bringing us home."

Lady Salisbury gasped.

Scarlett stared in front of her during this interchange on the downfalls of servants, picking at the sole on her plate, and wishing for the dinner to be over.

I would as soon have servants' company than yours right now, that's for certain. What would they do without servants? That's a more practical discussion, I'm sure.

From the sudden silence, Scarlett became aware that she was being spoken to for the first-time during dinner, and that a response was due.

"Scarlett!" Mrs Henson slapped her hand on the table.

"Yes, Mama?"

"Lady Salisbury is speaking to you."

"Excuse me, Lady Salisbury," Scarlett said.

Lady Salisbury and Mrs Henson gave each other a significant look of knowing.

"Your mother was just telling me how you like to keep company with your maid. Well, it won't do. You are tainted by association, remember? Why, only now, you were barely paying attention, that is not society's behaviour at all. It will not do," Lady Salisbury said, shaking her head.

"Scarlett?" her mother said, indicating a reply was needed.

"I'm sure, Lady Salisbury," Scarlett whispered.

"As you mention Parsons Running, I'm reminded, apparently, the fire at the castle was caused because a servant left a candle burning," Lady Salisbury said. She sat back, clutching the edge of the table for support after telling such a shocking tale.

Scarlett fought hard for the rest of the evening to keep up a show of attention, though she wished herself miles away.

Once the ladies were alone in the drawing room, as was the custom after dinner, the conversation turned to the Simm's ball.

"Don't you worry, Lavinia. I'm sure I'll have your daughter ready with the proper etiquette before Lady Simm's ball. You'll see," Lady Salisbury said.

Mrs Henson nodded assent.

"We will go out riding tomorrow, Scarlett. If only this dreadful weather would clear up," Lady Salisbury said, lifting her pointed chin to glance out of the window.

"Certainly, Lady Salisbury," Scarlett heard herself say.

Mrs Henson removed herself to the corner of the room to stand before the pianoforte. "There's one accomplishment that gives me very little concern. That is her performance at the pianoforte. Scarlett is so accomplished in this respect, and she has an excellent voice. Wouldn't you agree?"

"Indeed, she does. That's the best accomplishment there is to attract a gentleman. What did I tell you?" Lady Salisbury said.

With the gentlemen joining them in the drawing room, Lady Salisbury requested to hear Scarlett play and sing at the pianoforte to practice before company.

An eruption of applause followed her performance.

As Scarlett retired to her room, thoughts of what she'd read in the ancient book, as well as what Lady Salisbury had said about the fire, whirled through her mind.

Had the fire really been an accident as everyone seemed to conclude?

CHAPTER THREE

Frank Lattimer dipped the nib of a quill into the ink as he wrote a letter to his Aunt Violet in the country. He cursed the blotches staining the page. London was far enough away from Violet not to be anxious about how she might scold him for his terrible handwriting.

He remembered Closings Castle as a kind of mosque. As a young boy, the name had seemed appropriate because it was closed off from the world of ordinary people, yet since he'd come of age, the idea of being a master of a vast estate suited his purpose in rediscovering his capabilities.

The damp logs crackled in the fireplace, causing him to look up. Staring into the embers made him shudder. In his memory, the cries of the servants filled the room as well as water swishing from buckets as they struggled to contain the flames. Then he remembered the whirling ground from his being hoisted onto tall shoulders and carried away from the sickening scene. The loud clatter from the carriage wheels drowned out his traumatic thoughts as the young boy got a farewell glance at the castle, the home that was now closed to him forever.

Frank was startled out of his musings by what appeared to be a crash. Turning abruptly, he found it was only the butler bringing in the tea he'd ordered moments before. The butler carried the tray to the desk, pouring him a cup. He then placed a slice of lemon on the side. He was dismissed with a nod.

With pursed lips Frank sipped the burnt orange liquid reminding him of a cup of sunset. He settled back in his chair. He stared out of the window with dark, knitted brows at the ladies and gentlemen on the bustling street. It was strange to think of the servants opening the doors on Closings after all these years. It made his shoulders sink, but at the same time, his pulse quickened when he imagined the circumstance.

AS HOPED, AT LEAST by Lady Salisbury, the following morning brought with it some sunshine amongst the clouds. Scarlett was free to accompany her riding. She rode on Cleverly, a beautiful docile, and elegant Cleveland Bay horse with a rusty-brown hue, and a coal-coloured mane.

They rode through the grounds of Buckley House, past the village, and entered the gates to Lord Salisbury's parkland estate that extended a thousand acres beyond the manor.

En route to Salisbury Manor, where they'd planned to alight for lunch, they met an old acquaintance of Lady Salisbury's. Catching up with the rider at one of the follies, they found she was also headed for the same destination. Lady Salisbury slowed the stallion to a trot to say a greeting to the rider. She was taken aback when recognition dawned upon her. "Why Violet Ellingham, is it you?" Lady Salisbury said.

"It is me, Lady Salisbury. I was about to call on you, and here you are," Mrs Ellingham said in a serene, but at the same time, powerful voice. Dark poodle curls were visible under her riding hat. Eyes with the depth of an inkwell glared at the beholder like an eagle waiting for its prey.

"What brings you here?" Lady Salisbury asked as they continued to trot toward the manor, leaving Scarlett to follow suit.

"My nephew has returned to Parsons Running to open the old place again. He wishes to settle in the country now he has turned five and thirty," Violet said.

Lady Salisbury leaned forward and patted her horse's neck. "Open up Closings. I see. That'll get the town talking, for Closings has not been lived in since the old Lattimer's days."

"I don't see what that has to do with it," Mrs Ellingham answered, her brow furrowed.

"People like to talk," Lady Salisbury said. She paused before adding, "He will want to marry, I suppose?" Without giving Violet a chance to reply, she stopped the stallion, and waited for Scarlett to catch up. When she did, Lady Salisbury introduced her. "This is Scarlett Henson, my friend Lavinia Henson's daughter, who has lived at Buckley House these ten years. She will be attending the Simm's ball in London. I wonder, will your nephew be there?"

Mrs Ellingham gave Scarlett a cold glare by way of a greeting and said nothing.

Scarlett kept up a steady gaze, concealing the unease that sprung up inside her.

"I imagine he will attend. He does as he pleases," Mrs Ellingham replied, averting her attention back to Lady Salisbury.

Scarlett could breathe again.

They trotted the rest of the way to the manor in silence until they reached the towering metal gates.

The stable boy, who was seen mucking out the yard, dropped his rake on catching sight of them, and ran towards the gates.

"Wilson. We have a guest joining us. Will you see to Mrs Ellingham's horse?" Lady Salisbury said.

"M'lady," Wilson said.

They alighted at the gate, and the horses they led away with the help of the manservant.

Carrying her top hat for riding, Lady Salisbury led her guests through the hall of the house with a bouncy vigour. Her voice echoed against the cold stone wall.

"So, how will you like living at Closings?" Lady Salisbury asked in a high-pitched tone, once they were settled in the drawing room with extensive walls and a tall ceiling.

Mrs Ellingham showed no discomposure at her question, yet she paused with a porcelain cup poised to her lips as though she was thinking carefully before she replied. "It's exhilarating, yet at the same time tinged with sadness when I think of the family gone. My nephew was but a boy when his parents were killed so tragically, so with no one to take over the running of the estate, it was left until Frank cared to take it on again."

Lady Salisbury, who wore a flowing riding skirt, crossed her legs and said, "You think now is the right time for him to do so?"

"He pleases himself to think so. He makes his own way, does Frank. He's a strong man. Circumstances have made him so. Even as his guardian, there isn't much I can tell him, Lady Salisbury," Violet said.

"He inherits a large fortune with the estate, I would understand?" Lady Salisbury said.

"That is so. As large, if not larger than your own." Mrs Ellingham's eyes roamed about the room.

Lady Salisbury glanced at Scarlett, revealing in her face that which was foremost in her mind. A rich gentleman, on the lookout for a wife.

Scarlett shuffled, dreading what was coming next, and imagining Mrs Ellingham as a terrifying mother-in-law.

Mrs Ellingham fixed her with a stern glare.

The ensuing silence almost became too much for Scarlett to bear. She already disliked the sound of this Mr Lattimer, even though the family tragedy had intrigued her. She was determined not to be bullied into marriage with a man she did not care for. "I am sure this news does not concern me in any way, Lady Salisbury," she said, to her own surprise, as she broke the silence in a calm, clear tone.

Lady Salisbury opened her mouth to remonstrate. She closed it again as she thought it would not do to cause a scene in front of Mrs Ellingham.

"I'm sure I never thought it did, Miss Henson. I would not want my nephew to marry a gold digger," came Mrs Ellingham's sharp, cold reply.

Scarlett immediately regretted the disclosure of her feelings, and she bit her lip to stop herself from screaming out her frustration.

"I'm sure there's been a misunderstanding. I'm sure I never meant. . ." Lady Salisbury was cut short by the shadow of Mrs Ellingham towering above her as she stood up from the carved walnut chair.

"I'm afraid, as lovely as I've found this meeting, I must be getting along, as there is some business I must see to," Violet said, her lip protruding.

"I. . . of course, Mrs Ellingham, I. . ." Lady Salisbury's voice trailed away, and she was visibly shaking, being unusually put out.

They waited in silence as Mrs Ellingham was shown out.

"Well, I see no call for that. I don't know what to make of her strange manner. She was never so before," Lady Salisbury said.

"I never meant to offend her, Lady Salisbury. I'm sorry," Scarlett said.

"Don't apologise, my dear. There's no excuse for rudeness from Violet. I wonder what the meaning of it is. I always said there was some strange business up at that castle."

"What happened after the fire, Lady Salisbury?"

"Violet took Frank Lattimer, who was about five years old, if I remember rightly, to her London home. She became his legal guardian. I'd not heard before their arrival it was to be opened again, and I usually get to hear such news well in advance. It was all very hushed up. Strange indeed." She sighed.

"It is strange. Why come back now?"

"Why, indeed?" Lady Salisbury stared at the cream carpet. "Don't think you're completely let off the hook, though Scarlett. That Mr Lattimer is a good match for you. I'll be sure to tell your parents so," she added, making eye contact as she tapped her finger with every syllable.

"Because he is so rich?" Scarlett sighed.

"Money is the only consideration that counts in the end."

As usual, Lady Salisbury had the last word and the subject was dropped for the present time, much to Scarlett's relief.

CLOSINGS CASTLE, 1797

The road that wound from the path was dark. Violet clutched her suitcase, waiting on the steps outside the wrought iron gates of the castle attached to two pillars. She glanced tentatively at the numerous upstairs windows in the property. She didn't fear her sister. Isabella would never tell, but her husband would alert the whole house. If that should happen, she would never be able to hold her head high above the servants again. She would simply vanish into the night. That would be the best course of action for everyone concerned after what she'd done. She just had to escape her sister's husband.

A clatter of carriage wheels made her spin around. Violet rolled her eyes. "Drat, Lady Salisbury," she muttered as a hand waved to her from inside.

That woman has given herself airs since she married her lord.

The carriage halted with a screech, and Jane Salisbury put her head out. "Rather a dark night to be out, Violet." She cast her eyes over the suitcase.

The sound of snoring from her drunken lord slumped opposite her, drifted out.

Excuses raced through Violet's mind. "I'm staying with a friend in London. Why are you out so late yourselves?"

"We've been to a ball."

"Very swell," Violet said.

"It was our debut gathering as a married couple. My husband is so accomplished at dancing the waltz. We could have stayed all night."

"How fortunate. Were the Lattimer's not invited?" Violet was taking great pains to sound casual, though inwardly she feared the truth would come out.

"Ah, here's the problem: It was family only."

"Oh. Then, your first proper gathering will be here at the Closings annual ball?"

"Indeed, it shall. We're so eagerly awaiting that."

Lights came on in every room. Had the sound of the carriage alerted the house? Now, what would she do?

CHAPTER FOUR

It wasn't long before Mr Lattimer came up in conversation at Buckley House. Scarlett knew she could always rely on Lady Salisbury's discretion. In fact, he was raised during dinner the very next day by Mrs Henson. "Lady Salisbury was telling me some interesting news today at eleven, John," she said.

"What is that my love?" her husband asked, peering above a letter he had been perusing.

"Closings is inhabited again by the heir, Mr Frank Lattimer. He has come to settle in the country," Mrs Henson said.

"Is that so?" Mr Henson cast aside the letter.

"And that's not all," she said, waving a butter-laden knife at him.

Mr Henson remained silent, nervously spreading his hands on the white tablecloth.

"Well?" his wife asked, her sharp eyes piercing him through.

"Hm?" he asked, staring into space.

She finally began to butter a roll and said, "He inherits a very large fortune, much larger than Lady Salisbury's."

"Is that so? But I don't see. . ."

"Why, it's Scarlett's business, naturally. I'm sure he will wish to marry, for there must be a mistress in these great houses."

"Oh, Mother. We have not even met this Mr Lattimer yet," Scarlett said from her left, turning pale.

"Hush, Scarlett. Don't you want us to be more influential? You cannot be selfish and please yourself all the time. You must take him as he is," Mrs Henson said.

Scarlett glanced at her father with wide eyes. She would have greater success with him, as he was usually the more lenient of the two.

He simply shrugged his shoulders.

"What do you say to inviting Mr Lattimer and his aunt for dinner? John, dear. We must do so before Mrs Kettering does, for when Catherine comes home, she is sure to throw her at him. She likes to be the first at everything," Lavinia said.

Mr Henson only shrugged in agreement, fearing a dispute if he did otherwise.

"The aunt is rather frightening, Mama," Scarlett said, creasing her brow.

"According to Lady Salisbury, she is a very strong lady, that's all. I cannot fault her for that. I'm sure she will be very charming when you get to know her," Mrs Henson said.

"Lady Salisbury has changed her tune from yesterday. She said Mrs Ellingham had changed somewhat from when she first knew her, and that her manner was strange," Scarlett said.

"I know, dearest. But she said to me that despite her first misgivings about her, she thought better of it as it is too good a connection not to maintain," Lavinia said.

You mean, he is so rich.

There seemed to be no way she could escape his acquaintance. But Scarlett had to admit she'd like to have her curiosity about Frank settled.

Therefore, she had mixed feelings when Mr Lattimer and his aunt arrived at Buckley House a week later. Their engagement in more important matters made it impossible for them to grace their table earlier.

Mrs Ellingham gave her the same cold glare as they were introduced by Harper.

Mr Lattimer, who seemed to be a very haughty and cold man like his aunt, scarcely spoke a word the whole evening. When he did speak, it was in a ringing voice, loud and clear like a bell that the room couldn't help but pay attention to.

He had a strong resemblance to his aunt with unruly raven-coloured curls and the eyes of a windstorm that looked straight through you. Fair-skinned with defined cheekbones. If you looked closely, a small scar was visible under his left ear. His attire was minute to every detail, consisting of a dark coat, a cravat covering his neck, and light trousers. To Scarlett's perception the day wear always made men appear rougher and Frank was no exception to this rule.

Scarlett shivered as his lips brushed her hand on their first being introduced. She wasn't sure if this was because his eyes reminded her of his aunt's or not, but so it was.

She was wearing one of her finest evening gowns of beige muslin. She enjoyed how the lower, triangle cut of the neckline made her figure stand-out. Naima had set her hair in ringlets coiled around her face with height at the crown and parted in the centre.

After dinner, she was placed to the right of Mr Lattimer on the arched sofa while Mr Henson was placed on his left, attempting to engage him in conversation. "Do you care for golf, Lattimer?" he asked.

"Not especially," Frank replied, crossing his legs.

"Do you ride, sir?"

"I am not a rider. No."

"Oh, well you must go out riding with Scarlett. She is awfully good. She can teach you," Mrs Henson said while there was a pause in her conversation with Mrs Ellingham about furnishings.

"No. I thank you, Mrs Henson," Mr Lattimer said, his expression darkening.

"My nephew learnt to ride as a small boy. I'm quite sure he doesn't need Miss Henson's assistance," Mrs Ellingham explained.

"I beg your pardon," Mrs Henson said with a smile.

Scarlett's face flushed. There was a long pause, during which time Scarlett sensed Mrs Ellingham's gaze upon her, and she was sure there was little friendliness in it.

"Scarlett, why don't you play and sing for us?" Mrs Henson asked to defuse the situation.

"Of course, Mother," Scarlett said, glad of the diversion.

Scarlett moved slowly across to the pianoforte and began a favourite melody. She didn't notice how Mr Lattimer became unusually animated when she began to sing, and how he stared at her during the whole performance. His aunt noticed it, however, with alarm and contempt.

As Harper showed their guests out, Scarlett witnessed a hushed conversation as she was standing close to the door. It decided her opinion of Frank Lattimer once and for all.

"To think what people have told me of Lavinia Henson's upbringing, and she is trying to fling her daughter at you," Mrs Ellingham said.

Mr Lattimer gave a low chuckle. "She certainly hides the degradation well, but we both know their family is tainted by it."

It came as no surprise to Scarlett to hear Mrs Ellingham's words. Had she not always made her dislike known? She was more surprised at Frank, who seemed to give the impression that a match amongst them might not be unwelcome. She found herself very confused by his manner towards her, but she wasn't ready to admit it was her pride that instantly decided her against him. She knew for certain that she would do everything to avoid the union her mother desired with all her heart.

WHEN FRANK FIRST ARRIVED at Buckley House, meeting new acquaintances was daunting to him, especially when Scarlett was presented to him by her mother as a possible suitor. His fumbling for her hand made him afraid he had given her a bad impression of him. The result was a stunted conversation. He was ill at ease all evening until Miss Henson began to sing. It was the best moment of their visit. His frustration had shown itself in the hurried conversation with his aunt on their way out. Reflecting on it now, he was relieved none of the family had overheard what he said. Harper might have, but he wouldn't tell them.

Violet raised the subject of Frank's seeming interest in Scarlett when they were alone again and settled in the carriage home. "The Henson's are mercenaries, Frank. I could hardly keep my countenance with the way they tried to fling Miss Henson at you. She was having none of it at Lady Salisbury's, I can tell you," she said.

"Is that so?" he replied.

"You don't believe me?"

"I don't know if I do. It is quite common, you know? For influential families to want to marry their daughters to rich men."

"You wouldn't mind then, marrying a gold digger?"

"I wouldn't mind it from Miss Henson. I rather like the girl, even with her unfortunate relations. She would make a fine adornment at Closings, that's for sure," Frank said.

"But Frank, remember? We can't be too careful whom we let into Closings."

"She won't be just anyone, though, will she? She will be my wife, and she will want to keep the secret as much, if not more so than we do, to avoid ruining her family," Frank said.

"You can hardly speak sense right now, Frank. We will talk about it when you have sobered up, and you're less tired."

They rode the rest of the way home in silence.

Mrs Ellingham wrung her hands as she peered out on the road ahead.

Frank's mind took a more agreeable turn than he had openly conveyed to his aunt. He meditated on the great pleasure Scarlett would bring to Closings, and how such a fine woman would be a perfect match for the estate. To his aunt, marriage was a cold undertaking based on fortune. He was powerless to fight against her will as much as he desired to openly confess himself in love, a feeling he hardly dared to admit even to himself, because it meant he would have to hold nothing back. There were areas of his life he couldn't, under any circumstances, disclose without ruining his future prospects.

CHAPTER FIVE

One person Frank did allow himself to befriend was Julian Slater, whom he frequently visited at his townhouse in London, though his friend was never allowed to return the favour and visit Closings. In fact, Julian frequently teased his friend for the mystery he insisted on keeping about the castle.

Julian lived in an apartment on the fourth floor.

"Ah, Lattimer. I hear I am to congratulate you on winning the affections of a great beauty," Julian said.

Frank settled his shoulders into the undulating curve of a chair and crossed his legs. He was shaking his head as he said, "Country ways are unbelievable. Whatever put that idea into their heads? We have made no agreement."

Julian brushed his fair, floppy fringe away from his forehead, and laughed. He draped an arm along the chunky mantel shelf. "It all seems very stiff and upper class in the country, doesn't it? London is far more lenient when it comes to such matters of the heart. Yet, Scarlett Henson is a fine girl, and I repeat, a great beauty."

"Yes. You don't need to tell me. But you know my aunt," Frank said.

Julian's clear blue eyes took on an offended gleam. "Oh, the aunt. She objects to me, that's the reason she won't have me over at Closings."

To put off his reply Frank's eyes roamed, catching the carved feet of a bureau. As a boy he was petrified by such detail in his aunt's London home as they always reminded him of lion's paws.

Prising his eyes away from them, his tone rose a few notches as he said, "I told you to leave Closings out of it."

"All right. Don't get too spiky with me today. As a matter of fact, I've got an invitation for you."

Frank looked up, his hands clutching the chair. "What? Where to?"

"A young lady named Catherine Kettering has asked me to join her. It wouldn't hurt you to get out more often, and the best part is, she is a friend of Miss Henson..." Julian began.

"I know who she is," Frank said.

Julian left his place by the fire and went to a dresser in the corner, taking a neatly folded invitation out of one of the drawers. He came back to Frank's side, handing him the beige paper scrawled with ink. "I've persuaded her to let you accompany me. She is the kind of girl who would do anything for a friend."

Frank glanced at the writing on the paper and stuffed it in his breast pocket. "I can't go."

"You must. Can't you see it's a chance for you to spend time with Scarlett without the watchful hawk eyes of your aunt or Mrs Henson peering at you from every corner?"

Frank lowered his eyes. "I can't say it will do any good."

"You're fond of the girl, though, aren't you?"

"In my way, yes."

"Then here's your opportunity to prove it to her, and to deepen her affection for you in the process."

"She feels none," Frank said.

"Are you sure?" Julian asked.

"Quite sure."

"Yet, she barely knows you," Julian said.

"It will be a good match for her. I'll give her the credit to have the sense to work that out," Frank said.

"Still, you must try to woo her before it is too late."

"I can't promise anything," Frank said, tapping his breast pocket where he had safely tucked the invitation.

THE NEWS OF CATHERINE Kettering's return to town left Scarlett dashing about the house, her excitement bubbling over until she could almost burst. She basked in the knowledge that she would have someone to share her concerns about her parent's desire to see her wed on so early an acquaintance. It seemed like a long wait until she would see her at the card party.

Although it was a smaller model and different than Buckley House, Catherine's family estate was equally as grand with lots of windows like eyes peering at you. The card room held a sense of forbidden masculine presence, and it was exciting to feel like an outlaw for an evening. A grand pianoforte stood in the extended area of the room that Scarlett itched to play.

When Catherine gave her the news of Frank's being invited to their little card party, Scarlett never thought he would show.

She was distracted by the tall stature and large, grey eyes of a gentleman of good standing in the community named Romone Martin. Scarlett admitted she was overcome by his entertaining personality.

While the others played cards at the round table, Julian Slater joined Scarlett at the pianoforte. He turned the pages on the music, while watching for signs of his friend's carriage.

Mixed with the soft music was the sound of shuffling cards, as well as peels of triumph.

After Julian made known to her his close acquaintance with Frank, Scarlett was shocked he should have any friends at all.

As her fingers flung across the keys, she kept peering out of the window for signs of Frank. She wished to satisfy her curiosity as to how he behaved amongst a small gathering of friends. Perhaps she would learn more of his true nature while he was alone.

When his carriage finally drew up outside, she didn't know what to make of the strange tingling sensation in her hands. She was forced to abandon the playing, much to the complaint of the guests in the other half of the room.

"Why has the music stopped?" A guest asked.

"We have a new arrival," Julian answered, patting Scarlett's shoulder.

Frank strolled in, standing before the piano. A breeze blew the sheets of music into the air, sending a shiver down Scarlett's spine.

"Frank. I thought you'd never come," Julian said, the gladness showing on his face as they vigorously shook hands.

"My aunt is not easy to escape," Frank said, his jaw tightening.

"How did you manage to get past her?" Julian asked.

"She has retired for the night," Frank said.

"Here is Miss Scarlett," Julian said, pushing them closer together.

Scarlett raised herself from the piano stool, backing away from Frank. From a distance they stared dumbly at each other until one of them made a move to speak.

"Do you play cards, Miss Henson?" Frank asked, running fingers through his hair.

"I can tonight," she said hoarsely.

"I warn you, he's quite proficient," Julian whispered with a warm smile.

"I agree," Frank said, puffing out his chest.

Scarlett pressed her lips together, dragging her feet as they joined the others. Frank, though, walked with a confident air, hands on his hips.

They sat at a two-seater table.

Julian took up his place at the piano to serenade them with music.

They began in silence, Scarlett struggling to keep up with Frank's skill and a quick hand.

"Julian is nice. He seems to be a very gentlemanly man," Scarlett said, once she'd caught up with the pace of the game.

"Unlike me, I suppose you'd like to add?" Frank said, frowning down at the cards in his hand to work out his next move.

"No, indeed. It was simply an observation of your friend's character. I don't really know you enough to..." She paused.

"To dislike me, yet you do."

"Can you blame me when you take an obvious dislike to the name of Henson?"

"Yes, I'm not pleased with the name. It's American and your mother's upbringing is far from ideal, from what I've heard."

Her fingers clenched at his words. She misplaced some cards and they fell to the floor. She leaned down to retrieve them. "My mother is a lady," she said when she faced him again.

"She pretends to be," Frank said.

"Nonetheless, her marriage to my father made her so," Scarlett said.

A long silence followed.

Scarlett slammed the cards on the table.

"I'm trying to work out my next move," Frank said, brow furrowed.

"It's men like you who give money a bad name." Unwittingly her tone had grown louder. She realised the fact when a hush ascended in the room, and she noticed the other guests were enjoying the debate immensely.

"You don't think we should act superior?" Frank asked.

"There is no need for it. The poor are already painfully aware of their situation, we don't need to rub it in," Scarlett said.

"We have to carry ourselves in a certain style to give off a vibe of good breeding," Frank said.

"Thats what they'd have you believe. It's not the way I see it," Scarlett said.

Romone came over, leaning on Scarlett's chair and said, "Scarlett is a gem amongst women. Status could never change that."

She didn't notice how Frank's nostrils flared when he observed them. The connection between them couldn't be missed.

"What would you know about it?" Frank said.

"I'm a gentleman, the same as you are," Romone said.

"It's a pity you don't know how to behave like one," Frank said.

Scarlett dived out of her chair, spilling cards all over the floor. "Romone, I'd like you to accompany me home. I haven't had a chance to send for my carriage."

"With pleasure," Romone said throwing a triumphant grin at Frank.

Frank's expression soured as he watched them leave.

AFTER LEAVING THE KETTERING Mansion, Romone helped Scarlett to replace her delicate paisley shawl. They enjoyed a tranquil stride through the dimly lit village. As they reached the entrance to Buckley House, Scarlett paused. "Won't you come in?" she asked.

Romone blew on his cold hands. "Don't mind if I do."

The Henson's were delighted with their visitor. They'd entertained his parents on many occasions, and he was well liked in the village. Mr Henson got on particularly well with him.

After Romone left, Mr Henson nudged Scarlett in the ribs. "Romone Martin will make a good match for someone," he said, raising his pitch as his eyes sought out those of his wife.

Scarlett's face beamed.

Mrs Henson's eyes narrowed. Her lip curled sourly as she said, "He's handsome all right, but he's not that rich."

"He's tolerably well off," Mr Henson said.

"He doesn't own a castle," Lavinia said.

"There are more important considerations," Scarlett said.

Mrs Henson got to her feet as she said, "I'll hear no more of this nonsense. I'm going to bed."

CHAPTER SIX

"Scarlett, I cannot tell you how good it is to be back in Stanton Moore again, and to have your company, of course. I have missed having someone to tell my secrets to. I hardly had a soul in the world to talk to in London, apart from my horrible aunt. Why are aunts so disagreeable?" Catherine Kettering gushed when she met with Scarlett in the village to purchase ball gowns.

Scarlett could not stop a smile from appearing on her lips at Catherine's reference to aunts. "I confess I'm glad of your company too, dear Catherine. Apart from your little party, I have had to endure Lady Salisbury's company for most of the week, and she is worse than any aunt," Scarlett said, raising an eyebrow.

"How tiresome for you," Catherine said, inclining her head. She turned to her as they sauntered along the road.

As it was a chilly spring day, the girls both wore navy pelisse coats and straw bonnets with wide brims and ribbons tied under their chins.

"My mother and she would like to turn me into a great lady and have me married to Mr Lattimer of Closings. I'm afraid I must prove a disappointment to them both."

"Don't say so, Scarlett. You will make a great lady. As to the latter, I would avoid it at all costs. Mr Lattimer has not been at Closings above a month, and already there is a strong dislike of him," Catherine said, a creased brow overshadowing her plain features. "You saw evidence of it at our card party."

Scarlett nodded. “Speaking of which, I cannot tell you how much I like Romone.”

Catherine smiled. “He is a distinguished-looking man.”

“His conversation is well rounded out,” Scarlett said.

“And exciting,” Catherine said, laughing.

Walking a little way forward, Catherine’s brow wrinkled with concern. “Seriously, Scarlett...”

“Don’t trouble yourself, Catherine,” Scarlett interrupted, “you know me too well to doubt that I will not let myself be overpowered by my parents’ wishes.”

“I think I can reassure myself on that score. You always were headstrong,” Catherine said.

“What a strong word,” Scarlett said.

There was a pause.

“Has your family met Mr Lattimer properly?” Scarlett asked.

“Yes, my mother invited them to drink tea with us yesterday. I found them both very disagreeable indeed. My mother did also,” Catherine replied breathlessly.

“Me too,” Scarlett said.

Catherine paused, becoming serious when she spoke again. “Would you consider marrying him, though, Scarlett? Even if he is so rich.”

“It would only be to irritate his aunt.”

“Oh Scarlett. That would not be a good reason at all.”

“No, she’s shown such a pointed dislike of me that it’s good I’m only in jest,” Scarlett said.

“How can she be displeased with you?” Catherine asked.

“She feels that I’m a gold digger, which is true from my mother’s point of view, but it would hardly make any difference what I do.”

They had reached the boutique by this time. The shop was full, putting an end to their conversation.

“Can I be of assistance?” Mrs Lacey asked.

"We would like to choose some fabric for our ball gowns," Catherine replied.

"Certainly, Miss Kettering. The mauve silk is one of the most outstanding fabrics around. It hails from Paris," Mrs Lacey said, rolling a little of the fabric onto the counter in front of them.

"I do admire it," Catherine said, stroking the crisp material.

"The colour will set off your complexion well, Catherine," Scarlett said.

"I agree. I always think it goes very nicely with dark hair," Mrs Lacey said, picking up a piece of Catherine's chestnut waves.

"Can you have it made up for me?" Catherine asked.

"I will take your measurements." She showed them some sketches of the gown with wide sleeves and a slimline bodice.

Nodding her approval, Scarlett selected some rose pink and cream cotton. They then picked some other purchases to complete their outfits and headed out into the street.

"Obviously, anyone who is anyone is vying for Mr Lattimer to marry them. He is so influential, as well as rich, that his manners are of no consequence," Catherine said as they were seated in the window at a café.

"So, my mother keeps on saying," Scarlett said as she poured tea into a cup.

"He will be at the ball, and no doubt all the ladies will wish to dance with him," Catherine said.

"They are welcome to him. I shan't be vying for his attention, that is certain, despite my mama," Scarlett said with finality.

When Scarlett arrived back at Buckley House, she was surprised to see Mr Lattimer's carriage waiting outside. She knew it was his as the gold crest depicting a castle was unmistakable and his manservant was standing by the carriage, staring at her as she walked by.

When she reached the front door, it opened, and as Harper stepped back, Mr Lattimer himself appeared in a hurried motion. They almost collided in the doorway until Scarlett stepped back, squashing herself up against the door frame to avoid him. He tipped his hat and carried on in silence, his arm brushing against her shoulder.

What could he be doing here?

Turning to Harper, she said out loud, "Where is my father, Harper?"

"He's in the library, miss. He's asked not to be disturbed."

"Thank you, Harper. What was Mr Lattimer doing here?" She was not expecting a reply, and none came, except his usual shrug of the shoulders.

Folding her arms, she went up to her room to change for lunch.

Mr and Mrs Henson were unusually quiet over lunch, and Scarlett watched their faces with narrowed eyes.

They would not give anything away.

The only thing she noticed was that her father looked grave. She suspected it had something to do with Mr Lattimer's visit. She dared not raise the subject.

I will find out soon enough, I have no doubt.

MR LATTIMER QUITE LIKED the challenge Scarlett had put to him at the card party of winning her over, of gaining the victory over Romone.

He could see why Scarlett would be swayed into accepting his rival's proposal if he didn't act soon to secure her affection. His conversation was lively, even mesmerising. Those reasons are what prompted his visit to her father. He mulled over his decision as he took the country air on a long walk, next to a walled garden. Walking was a chance to be alone, and to contemplate the world. He found great comfort from sometimes being on his own, at one with nature.

At a clearing, he approached an old oak tree, and paused to take a breath whilst contemplating a deep valley tinged with a hint of autumn.

Shielding his face with his hands, he craned his neck to get a closer look at a low-flying buzzard until he flew out of sight, carried on the wind, and Frank moved along also.

As he made the trip back to his residence, he met Julian Slater coming up the hill. Fear pulsated through him at the sight of his friend so near to the castle walls.

"What on earth are you doing here?" Frank said as he met him halfway.

"Your enthusiasm doesn't suit you," Julian said, grinning.

"I hope you don't expect me to invite you in. My aunt's at home."

"It seems a shame as I'm so close. But no, I came to tell you farewell. I'll be out of your hair for a long while, so you needn't worry I shall repeat this trip. I'm joining the navy. I've finally signed up," Julian said.

"I'm glad for you. I hope it works out well, though I will miss having an ally."

"I'm sure you'll manage well enough without me. It's a shame I won't be around to witness the debates between you and Miss Henson. Or a duel with that Romone character. I suppose that can't be helped," Julian said.

"No indeed. I'm sure nothing will come of it, mind you," Frank said.

"You never can tell," Julian said.

They shook hands on it and walked in the opposite direction from the castle together.

CHAPTER SEVEN

Scarlett didn't find out the purpose of Mr Lattimer's visit until before the Simm's ball. A party of guests, which included the Henson's, arrived at Shelby Abbey, where the ball was to be held a week before it began.

About an hour after the Henson's arrival at the abbey, Scarlett and Naima were in one of the lofty rooms of great quantity, setting out gowns and admiring the view of the regimented grounds from the window, when Mrs Henson entered, and dismissed Naima.

When Mrs Henson settled on the bed, patting the space beside her, Scarlett became uneasy at the serious look on her face. "Sit down beside me for a moment, Scarlett, my dear. I have something to say to you," she said.

Scarlett obeyed, serenely placing her hands one on top of the other with palms facing upwards as she had been trained to do by Mrs Simpkins, her governess. The woman had been strict, but she had known her place.

Scarlett attempted to hide her unease with a gentle smile.

"Now Scarlett, I want you to be good to Mr Lattimer when he arrives for the ball. It is due to him after his kindness to you," Mrs Henson began.

Mr Lattimer was staying with his aunt in London, who would not be joining him at the ball.

"His kindness? Well, I have not seen any evidence of that, and I'm sure it is a quality with which he is sadly lacking," Scarlett said.

"You must not say so, Scarlett, for I meant his kindness in noticing you, my dear. He visited with your father about a month ago to propose himself as a suitor for your hand. Your father accepted. . ." Mrs Henson broke off, placing her hand over Scarlett's to prevent her from wringing them together. "The engagement will not be announced until after the ball, as that will be your coming out party. He will keep it secret until then."

"And am I to have no say in the matter?" Scarlett asked.

Mrs Henson shook her head. "A lady doesn't generally refuse when a gentleman of his calibre asks for her hand. It's a matter of obligation under such circumstances. It's her duty to her family to accept him."

"But Mama, how could you and Father agree to this? You know he is a cold-hearted man."

"Hush. You must not say so, for he will be your husband. You must resign yourself to this before you see him. That's why I've told you tonight, so you can act cordially towards him," Mrs Henson said, holding Scarlett's face between her hands.

"I cannot be his wife, Mama."

"I'll hear no more arguments on the matter. It is a good match for you."

"Mama, please. Is there anything you want me to do? I can improve my behaviour in society if you point me in the right direction and I don't have to marry a man I know nothing about. At least allow me some time." All this Scarlett begged before her mother on her knees, from an anguished heart.

Mrs Henson remained unmoved. "Scarlett, this marriage will help you improve your etiquette. I can't take you any further. When you're the mistress of a great house, you will understand."

"But Mama, Mr Lattimer doesn't exactly approve of our family. Don't you have any pride? His aunt accuses us of gold-digging. I can't play a part in our family name being dragged through the mud. More investigation is needed into the Lattimer's intentions."

Lavinia's chin rose. "Of course, I've got my pride. That's why I want this for you." She stroked her daughter's hair. "There goes the gong for dinner. Let's go down together."

Scarlett feigned obedience for the present time, and they went down to the dining room arm in arm.

When they arrived downstairs, the mahogany table that graced the dining room was full of guests. The Earl of Simms and Lady Simms seemed a long way from the entrance at the head of the table. He was a chubby, bald man, of five and sixty while his wife, a good five and twenty years younger, was small and slender with shrew-like pointed features, and caramel-coloured hair.

Scarlett and Mrs Henson found their places at the table beside Mr Henson, who glanced concernedly at Scarlett to see how she had taken the news.

"How are you?" he whispered in her ear.

She reached out and squeezed his hand in reply, to which he smiled.

"Are you resigned?" he asked.

"I'm not sure about any of this, Father," she replied, glancing nervously at her mother. "I'm resigned for now because I wouldn't want to cause a scene, but if there's a way to convince Mama, let us do so together."

"Don't say something you might think better of in the morning, my love. Who knows that you might not grow to like Mr Lattimer? He has a kind of charm, don't you agree? He has Closings Castle to recommend him to you," Mr Henson said.

Scarlett glanced across the table to Mr Lattimer. That he was charming, she couldn't deny, but it was the kind of charm rich men have who are pleased with themselves, and their situation. He had a way of holding himself in an upright posture that spoke volumes of his wealth and influence in society.

She nodded somewhat unwillingly, and they turned their attention to the earl, who was about to give a speech.

After dinner, the ladies each took turns exhibiting their skills at the grand pianoforte in the music room.

"I must say I'm impressed with your daughter, Lavinia. Such skill at the pianoforte, and so elegant, and pretty. She will make a great match someday," Lady Simms said, sitting beside Mrs Henson.

"Thank you, Elaina. I'm awfully proud of her," Lavinia said.

"Of course, you are. She will be a favourite at the ball."

"I think she will," Lavinia said, giving her a tight-lipped smile.

"Lavinia? Is there something I should know?" Lady Simms asked.

"I believe she will be very soon engaged to a very rich gentleman. That is all I can tell you for the present."

"Hm, indeed. You know I wouldn't breathe a word if you were to tell me the gentleman's name."

"I know I can rely on your discretion, Lady Simms, but I can't tell you anymore as I am sworn to secrecy."

"In that case, I shall not press you any further on the subject. What is her gown like?" Lady Simms asked.

"It is quite sublime," Lavinia said, going on to describe the silver ball gown with long lace sleeves.

"That will do nicely," Lady Simms said.

"MISS SCARLETT," NAIMA said through Scarlett's bedroom door at the abbey.

There was no answer, but the maid thought she could hear weeping coming from within.

"Miss Scarlett. Would you like me to help you prepare for bed?" Naima asked, pretending not to notice there was anything wrong.

"If you wish," came Scarlett's reply through sobs.

Naima tiptoed about the room. She was moved by the sight of Scarlett lying on her bed with swollen eyes and a crumpled dress. The maid looked concerned and busied herself with finding a nightgown from the wardrobe. She swung the clothes from side to side in her anguish.

"You need not be concerned, Naima. I'm fine."

"Forgive me, but you don't look well at all. I can see the trace of your tears, as they used to say back in Ireland. I won't ask what could have happened as it wouldn't be right in my position."

"Why would it not be right? We're friends, aren't we? Naima."

"I am a servant, miss." On finding a suitable nightgown, Naima spread it out on the bed. She smoothed it out with her fists.

"You sound like Mama. You are more than a servant to me, Naima."

"Nay. It cannot be so," Naima said.

"They're trying to make me Mr Lattimer's wife. There, I have said it. Whether you wish to know it or not," Scarlett said.

"Who says so?"

"My mama and pa. He is not happy about it, I'm sure. It's all arranged without me," Scarlett said.

"Couldn't you refuse?"

Scarlett played with her hair. "You know the rules. A lady is under obligation to accept when a gentleman asks her."

Naima nodded sadly.

Scarlett's face hardened. "But I mean to put up a fight."

"You're sounding more like yourself. I'm sorry for you. It's hard for you to have to make such a choice. Anyone who speaks against your family must be bad. I'm sure of it. I'm sad there's nothing I can do," Naima said.

"I'm grateful for your concern."

Naima reached her side, squeezing her hand. "I'll always be here for you. I can promise you that."

Scarlett smiled as she returned the pressure on her hand. The good old maid scored a ten for trying, but Scarlett wondered how she could ever fulfill her promise.

AS MORNING DAWNED OVER the abbey, Scarlett wrote a note addressed to her mother and father, proposing a family meeting in her room before breakfast.

Slipping out, she posted it under the door of the bedroom they slept in.

"My dear. Why have you called us here? I thought it was all settled?" Lavinia said as they bustled into her room an hour later.

"Please be seated," Scarlett said, standing by the bed with her hands clasped in front of her.

Mrs Henson sat at the dressing table while her husband stood by her side.

Mr Henson put his hand on his wife's shoulder. "Hear her out. It's her future, after all," he said, holding his head high.

"Father is right, Mama. This has gone on long enough. I can't stay silent anymore." Scarlett clenched her hands into fists by her sides.

"You're not telling me you mean to refuse Mr Lattimer after his generosity to you?" Lavinia asked.

"I mean I will not be bullied and cajoled into making a hasty decision. Should I choose to marry at all, it will be of my own volition," Scarlett said.

Mrs Henson gaped. "You're more of a fool than I thought. John, won't you try to persuade her?"

Mr Henson removed his hand from his wife's shoulder. "Not this time, my love. Let the responsibility rest with our daughter. She's more than capable. . ."

". . . Of causing a scandal. What will people say? How will I break it to Mrs Kettering? Better still, to Lady Simms?" Lavinia said.

"You don't owe them an explanation," Scarlett said.

Mrs Henson raised her chin. "Their opinions matter. They're the very foundations of high society. Do you wish to be an outcast? To be shunned and degraded in their eyes forever?"

Scarlett threw up her hands. "No. Anything but that."

"You only need to cast your mind back to Harriet Fincher to be aware of what happens to those who disregard societal norms," Mrs Henson said.

Scarlett hid her face. "Don't remind me."

A satisfied smile appeared on Mrs Henson's lips. She knew fear of the unknown was what scared her daughter more than anything. She'd worked that out early on in her life when their daughter was toddling about their estate, and she wandered too far from the gate. Screams of terror pierced the air until one of the maids found her and brought her home. "Harriet forsook her genteel position to marry a commoner. No one will even mention her name, let alone speak to her in the street. You too will be Jilted by anyone that matters," Lavinia said.

Scarlett stared at her feet.

Mrs Henson rose abruptly. She beckoned for her husband to follow her outside. "Let us leave her to stew over the matter. I'm certain she will make the correct choice once she's left to her own devices," she whispered to him.

CHAPTER EIGHT

The evening of the ball finally arrived.

Mr Lattimer strolled into the ballroom. He ran a finger along the high-necked collar on his evening shirt, wishing to be alone so he could loosen it. He looked as haughty and as pleased with himself as ever.

Perhaps more so with his recent conquest of my hand. Or so he thinks. Scarlett thought.

A silence ensued as the guests stopped to give him curious glances.

Gentlemen like Mr Lattimer didn't have to say something flattering to be noticed in a room full of strangers. He made his presence felt in the way he could take up the whole room as though he was the only person in it. Other guests either loved him for this type of charisma or hated him for it. Scarlett was inclined to the latter view even if she couldn't help but admit he had a class of distinction about him.

The time seemed to drag as she listened to her heart thumping in her chest. She tapped her feet as she struggled to count the steps of the first dance in her mind, for she knew he would ask her, and she blushed lest she should make a wrong move with the master of Closings of all people.

"Mr Lattimer. How nice to have you with us," Lady Simms gushed, rushing over to him.

"Lady Simms," he said in his low, deep voice. He took her hand, planting a kiss there.

"How is dear Violet?"

"My aunt is well. Thank you."

Scarlett managed to avoid his gaze from across the room as he spoke to Lady Simms. She found she could not do so for long as he eventually moved her way. As anticipated, he solicited her hand for the first dance.

"I would be honoured, sir," Scarlett replied.

Frank grinned before edging away to speak with the earl.

"Well, he didn't waste any time there, did he?" Catherine said, standing close by her.

Scarlett lowered her eyes, and whispered, "Hush. He may hear you."

"What if he does hear me? What is wrong with you? You act as though you were afraid of him."

"I can't tell you now. Come to my room this evening, and I will tell you all," Scarlett whispered.

Scarlett was called away as the first dance was about to begin. She took her position opposite Mr Lattimer with some trepidation, yet she viewed the occasion as an opportunity to question him further about his hopes regarding her, and to try to convince him to drop the pursuit of her hand. Scarlett praised the new trend of the Boulanger dance as the slow music meant she could speak to him freely.

They started the dance in silence. One was too pleased with himself to speak and the other was at a loss for words.

"Is your aunt in town?" Scarlett said to begin the discussion.

He looked surprised that she had spoken, but he answered politely enough. "Yes, Miss Henson. My aunt is in town."

"Do you know the Earl and Lady Simms well?" Scarlett asked, her elaborate curls bouncing with the movement of the dance.

"Not well at all. They are the sort of family one ought to keep in with." He held his chin high.

"Are you always so abrupt?" Scarlett asked. Anger at his haughty manner had made her bold.

"Do you always ask so many questions? What can you mean by it?" he asked after a short pause.

"I believe questions are used in general to get better acquainted with a person, and their character. I simply would like to know you better. As your future wife, I think that is necessary, don't you?"

"You wish to accept my offer?" he asked.

"I speak about ideals. If you insist on pursuing my hand, however, I must warn you, I think it is only right that you should know that I do not care for you at all. I must beg you to reconsider your offer," Scarlett said.

"Why no. I thank you for your concern, Miss Henson. The match, in terms of monetary considerations, is not bad. Your charm and beauty will make an excellent adornment at Closings. I, of course, know it to be only mercenary on your part," he said.

Scarlett's cheeks flushed. She was grateful to be concealed from his sight by other dancers as they intertwined and glided across her. She composed herself in time to face him again only to find he had a smug expression on his face.

"I wish to make myself perfectly clear, sir, with all due respect to you as a gentleman, that I do not wish to be your wife, with or without your wealth and influence that is so important to my family. I feel I have no choice, however, to accept your offer, if you will not withdraw it, based on obligation alone. I'm a person of principle, even if you are not," she said, her voice calm.

There came a low laugh from under his breath. "Thank you. That's all the assurance I need."

Scarlett's heart sank within her at his reply for she hoped to change his mind by the admission of her disfavour to the match, but his knowledge of her indifference only made him even more determined to win her.

The dance coming to an end meant they were forced aside. She watched her dance partner disappear into the crowd.

"What exquisite dancing, my dear," Mrs Henson said, seeking her out from the crowd.

"Honestly, Mama?"

"I didn't know you had it in you to be so elegant. It must be Mr Lattimer's doing. How well you look together," Mrs Henson said.

"Do you think so?" Scarlett asked, staring at the crowd.

"What did he say to you?"

"Nothing of consequence. Like I told you before, he has no respect for our family. I don't think he cares much about me."

"I won't listen to you," Mrs Henson said, covering her ears. She dashed away before Scarlett could offer any further objections.

Low in spirit, but still as determined as ever to ensure this disastrous marriage would never take place, Scarlett sauntered to the balcony, walking softly to the edge. She drew in a breath as Mr Lattimer's tall frame came into the light in the garden. At that moment, she could hardly recognise him. His upright posture was unusually downcast.

A young boy with patches sewn on his ragged trousers and who had bare feet thick with grime, his fingernails broken and dirty, seemed to be pleading with him.

Mr Lattimer turned his face, and as it met the light of the moon, the expression she read in those dark eyes, usually so cold, was softer. He pocketed his hand and drew out a handful of change, depositing it in the boy's upturned palms. The boy's eyes lit up in amazement. He ran away before the generous gentleman changed his mind.

Scarlett at once drew back and gasped.

How could the proud master of Closings Castle show such tenderness when he was inclined to it? Could it be he wasn't as bad as he made out when in the company of strangers?

A sudden sympathy for the boy's situation that was not so different from her own, crept up on her. It was, after all, her lack of cordiality in her own family life that was always such a sore spot with her growing up. Even when one is brought up high, there can be poverty when a lack of love and respect reigns.

Her mind flew back to her earlier interest in the Lattimer family and their home. She spared a thought for the people of Parsons Running. She wondered if her influence as a mistress might help them to gain the healing, they were so desperate for.

She couldn't pinpoint if this was the reason why, when his step was heard on the curved stone steps and he appeared on the balcony, she allowed him to stand close to her, and why, when he reached into his pocket, pulling out a diamond ring, she allowed him to slip it on her finger. He held it out to her, obscuring it from the view of the crowd within.

"Will you do me the honour of wearing this ring?" he asked.

She looked into his eyes, where there were still traces of the change, she'd seen in him. "If we're to form a partnership we're in it together. You must see that. We need to start acting like we are on the same side," she said.

"Are we on the same side?" he whispered.

Her lips parted. All that came out of them was a wisp of air instead of words. "We each need to make this match a success for the sake of Closings and the people who look up to the name of Lattimer," she managed to say.

He became wretched once more because of her sensible proposal, and as he kissed her hand, he promised to make things all right. "My aunt is the practical member of the family. I have more interesting reasons for wanting this match than money. You will be a grand show for Closings," he said.

And it was done. She didn't quite know how, but so it was.

He was gone almost as soon as they'd made the agreement.

Scarlett went to find her mother, and while she was still dazed from how it had happened, she held up her hand where the ring glistened in the light of the chandelier.

"Oh, how magnificent! A scarlet-coloured diamond in honour of your name. I was certain he was a romantic, generous man under all his visage," Mrs Henson said, and this consolation seemed to ease her guilt for a time.

BEFORE RETIRING TO rest, Frank roamed the gardens at the abbey. The engagement had given him a lot to think about.

The life he'd lived was reflected at him in the boy's eyes, and even though he was rich, the loneliness bore through him and tore him apart. He was ready to share his life with someone.

He had just passed by the huge monument in the centre of the lawn, when a rustle from the bushes startled him.

A gentleman approached him.

Frank stopped abruptly. "Lord Simms," he said as his face came into the light.

His Lordship placed a finger over his own lips. "Is that you, Lattimer?"

Frank confirmed that it was him, adding, "What are you skulking about out here for?"

"I needed to escape. I'm getting too decrepit for gatherings of this size," Lord Simms said, slapping Frank's back. "Let it be our little secret. Good at keeping secrets, are you?"

"Oh, yes. I can be discreet when it's called for," Frank said.

"Ha! That's the spirit. Are you a sociable man?"

"Not really, but my aunt insists upon it. We must keep up appearances, and all that."

"I know how aunts can be," His Lordship said.

"I find society tiresome and frivolous. There are much less tedious ways to spend an evening," Frank said.

"Except when drink is on offer, eh?" Lord Simms said with a wink.

"Yes, the tedium of many evenings can be gotten through with a glass of Port. However, I only come for the Vol-au-vents," Frank said with a chuckle.

"YOU ARE ENGAGED TO Mr Lattimer. It cannot be true. Oh, Scarlett, how could you do it?" Catherine said on becoming acquainted with the circumstance of her engagement. She was crouched on Scarlett's bed beside her.

"While the match was decided for me, you know me too well to doubt that I would have put up a fight already. You know it is a matter of obligation, but I wouldn't have accepted him on that basis alone. I fought to get him to change his mind about me. However, I have made up my own mind to accept his proposal tonight. I believe there is good in him. I think I can change him for the better," Scarlett said.

"Did you make that clear to him?" Catherine asked.

"I made sure he knew that I didn't care for him, but it did not change his mind."

Catherine's fingers stroked the bedclothes. "You always said he is such a bad man. What did his aunt have to say?"

"Only Mr Lattimer can answer that," Scarlett said.

"This news concerns me deeply, Scarlett. I danced with him this evening, and I found him very disagreeable and haughty. He will not be good to you, I'm sure."

"You must not speak against him, Catherine. He is to be my husband, after all."

"I wonder why you can be so resigned to it. I'm sure I would not be if it were me. How could your father agree to this?"

"He couldn't help it. Mr Lattimer is a man who cannot be refused. Yet it is done now. I believe it will work out well," Scarlett said.

"Oh, Scarlett. I'm sorry for you," Catherine said, giving her a gentle hug.

"Don't be, Catherine. I have nothing to complain about, really, and it is an honour to be chosen by someone such as him. I will live in comfort at Closings and never want for anything again. There are a lot of people in this world who can't boast of that."

"Dear, dear Scarlett. I know you will use your influence only for the good of others," Catherine said.

"I will try," Scarlett said.

The wind and rain howled through the abbey that night as doubts crept into Scarlett's mind about the suitableness of her choice of partner. Visions of herself with a heart turned to stone alongside her cruel husband in a black castle, ruling the servants like slaves, troubled her sleep. She tossed and turned in her bed until finally, giving up on sleep altogether, she slipped out of bed, and reached for her chemise nightgown.

She rushed to the balcony doors, flinging them open, and stepped out, teetering on the edge of the frame that leveled out onto the balcony beneath. The cool rain on her face was refreshing and numbed her troubling thoughts away.

When she pulled back inside, her face and hair were dripping wet. She found a towel from the bathroom, drying herself off. She settled on the chaise longue beside her bed, drifting into a deep sleep.

Flames engulfed the castle.

Scarlett struggled to free her dress from the handle of the door leading to safety, but it would not budge, and she was powerless to move.

Glass from the windows shattered all around her, and suddenly she heard the ceiling begin to groan above her head. She raised her arms to shield her face as it caved in.

She was awakened by someone gently shaking her. She peered up at Naima through bleary eyes, trying to move her legs. The ache stopped her. She shivered. The cold had gone right through her.

"Oh, Miss Scarlett, you're freezing. Come and warm yourself," Naima said, rubbing Scarlett's arms.

"Naima, I'm fine now," Scarlett insisted when she had warmed up a little, with Naima still rubbing her arms, and supplying her with hot coffee.

Naima, satisfied by this assurance, dressed her.

"What were you thinking of Miss Scarlett? You could have caught a chill," Naima gently scolded.

"I got up to watch the storm. I must have fallen asleep."

On being summoned by the gong, Scarlett rushed downstairs to the dining room. A mass of complaints of sleepless nights reached her ears as she entered. Only Mr Lattimer, who had stayed the night at the abbey, seemed unconcerned.

As she helped herself to a breakfast of eggs, pancakes and oysters from the sideboard, the maize yellow of her simple morning dress intensified as it caught the golden sunlight from the large window.

As she selected a chair beside Catherine, she pondered how Frank was never flustered. He was sitting quietly sipping his coffee next to the earl who was talking to him non-stop while he was not paying much heed to the conversation. Furthermore, he was equally unmoved by Scarlett's arrival in the room.

"Are you all right, Scarlett? You are pale," Catherine asked with a look of concern.

"It is only the storm. I hardly slept," Scarlett said.

"Nor I. It is creepy in a place like this," Catherine said.

"It's most inconvenient. Especially as a highly anticipated event makes it imperative that you get your beauty sleep, Scarlett," Mrs Henson said, cutting into the conversation just loud enough for Scarlett and Catherine to hear.

It seemed to Scarlett that her mother emphasised this fact for Catherine's benefit in hopes it would get back to Mrs Kettering.

The party left the abbey shortly after breakfast.

Mr Lattimer left for his aunt's London home to convey to her the news of his engagement.

The engagement was promptly announced in the newspaper on the morning of the Henson's arrival at Buckley House. There were exclamations of joy heard all over the building from Mrs Henson for the rest of the day.

Lady Salisbury paid a call on them in the afternoon to offer her congratulations. Also, to profess herself penitent for her earlier qualms about Mr Lattimer and his aunt.

CHAPTER NINE

With the wedding looming over their heads, Mrs Henson attempted to convince Scarlett of the rightfulness of her choice by inviting Mr Lattimer to dine with them.

Scarlett's heart could almost have burst out of her chest as Naima dressed her for the very important occasion.

"Mama has threatened to disown me if this falls through," Scarlett said as Naima wheeled around her, turning up the hem of her new dress.

"I expect she doesn't mean it. We all speak words we don't mean to carry out in the heat of the moment," Naima said.

Scarlett spoke to her over her shoulder. "I'm at a loss how to speak to him. I'm aware there's some good in him, but how do I go about drawing it out?"

Naima finished applying the last stitch to the bustle skirt, smoothing it out with a rustle. She patted her handiwork. "If anyone can do it, you can, miss. You have such a gentle way with you. You'll work it out," Naima said, lacing up the corset bodice.

Taking a final glance in the mirror as she smoothed her hair, Scarlett glided down the stairs, every step feeling like it was bringing her closer to disaster.

Her mother clasped her hands together in pride.

"You won't leave us alone right away?" Scarlett asked as her foot touched the bottom step. She grasped the banister.

Mrs Henson took her arm, pulling her off the step. "You will speak to him alone. You managed the engagement yourself, so you can manage him well enough on your own," she whispered.

Scarlett's protests were quieted when Mrs Henson pushed her into the room, closing the door on the two of them.

Mr Lattimer, who had his back to her, facing the fireplace, spun around when he heard the latch click. As he moved her way, there was an obvious admiration in his gaze, yet although they were so close, an imaginary precipice seemed to separate them at their feet. Neither of them dared to breathe in case they fell.

"Shall I play for you?" she asked hastily, shuffling towards the piano. Music had a way of covering awkward silences, and they could talk freely this way.

"I will turn the pages as Julian does so well," Frank said, following her.

"How is dear Julian?" she asked, positioning herself at the instrument, and flexing her hands to begin playing. The music book was open on her favourite Mozart Sonata, and she chose to perform this same piece tonight.

"He's due to travel soon. He's joining the navy," Frank said.

"Won't that be a sad loss for you? It helps to have some friends around us."

He eyed the back of her head in amusement at her reference to his lack of friends. "But not for my aunt. She didn't take too kindly to him."

"Nor to anyone." She bit her lip after speaking so openly about her dislike of his aunt. "I don't mean to be rude," she added.

"I'm not offended. My aunt can be put off very easily."

"She doesn't want you to marry me," she said.

"I have persuaded her otherwise," he said.

"I'm almost glad you did. I see now we'll make an ideal team, whatever our feelings for each other are," Scarlett said.

"I'm glad you've finally come to your senses. I don't believe you'll find a better match," he said.

"As long as we're on the same side and we can put old grievances behind us, the marriage should work well."

"I won't argue with you there. I'll try to make it work."

Scarlett cleverly turned the conversation to music, commenting on the way music was a fine accompaniment to any situation.

"I agree. The first time I heard you play at Buckley House was a turning point for me," Frank said.

"It helped settle my nerves on that occasion," Scarlett said.

His fingers almost brushed her cheek as he turned over the page on the music. "I must admit, I prefer music to be rousing. Somehow it spurs you on and often acknowledges the turmoil inside you."

"Yet, softer music can dispel those moods rather than encourage them," Scarlett said.

"I can see how, on some occasions, it might be wise to follow your advice. However, I'm determined to go with the turmoil for the present," he said.

LATER, WHEN SHE WAS in her room, Scarlett stared at her own reflection in the mirror at her dressing table. She recalled their conversation about music. It had become apparent tonight that she'd made the right decision by choosing to marry Mr Lattimer. They each offset their deficiencies, and even though she was still sure that no love resided in her heart toward him, she believed she'd found her calling.

Could it be it wasn't a coincidence that her curiosity had been raised about the castle?

The more she considered it, the surer she was that Closings Castle was where she belonged. With this assurance to herself, she blew out the candle, plunging her into darkness.

INSTEAD OF RETIRING to rest, Frank embarked on a brisk walk to prepare his mind for the major turn his life was about to take. The soft music Scarlett had played echoed in his mind, equaling his romantic mood. He was relieved to be assured of her promise before she could be swept away by Romone Martin's dazzling personality.

As he stared up at the stars, he hoped they could make it work, but this feeling was not long-lived. He knew too well how fleeting the heart could be, especially when any amount of distance weaved its way between two people, no matter how committed they were to each other.

Bowing his head, he covered his eyes. Last night's dream came back to him. Closings had been slipping away from his grasp like a slithering snake. How relieved he was when he'd awoken to find himself at the castle. He was drenched in a cold sweat that threatened to return to him tonight.

A sense of permanence came with his new role. He'd slipped into it exceedingly well. All that was missing was Scarlett.

CHAPTER TEN

The wedding took place on a warm, breezy day in the summer. The gathering was a greatly anticipated affair in the town of Stanton Moore. There was a buzz of excitement amongst the guests, many of whom had known Scarlett since childhood. They were all assembled to await the bride.

Lady Salisbury was nonetheless talkative. She chirped away excitedly to Mrs Ellingham, who sat beside her with a stony expression. Though they had got off to a rocky start, they'd since met up often and gone out riding together.

"I am thrilled for Miss Henson. It is such a fine match. I hope she will not find Italy too hot," Lady Salisbury said.

"Possibly. She is a peaky creature," Mrs Ellingham replied, her teeth clenched.

"The villa is quite airy, though?" Lady Salisbury asked.

"I imagine so," Violet said.

"It's a shame she won't be around as often. I'll miss our conversations. I shall have to content myself with occasional visits."

"What do you mean?" Violet asked.

Lady Salisbury fanned herself. "I don't mean to imply, Violet, that there is anything wrong with the distance, only, I should like to be near her to assist her in any way I can. It can be daunting, as experience has taught me, to become the mistress of a great estate such as Closings."

"With all due respect, the castle runs itself as the servants are long-standing and well-trained. I have implicit trust in them to see that things are run properly as I'm sure the future Mrs Lattimer is entirely incapable of doing," Violet said.

"Oh, I didn't mean she would not manage. I'm sure she will make a great lady. She has uncommonly improved under my supervision these past few months."

"Yes, but she is so young. Why he had to choose a girl so young is beyond me. I told him so when he announced the engagement, but he would not budge. He's always been one to be taken in by a pretty face."

"There's also her fortune. Let us not forget that Violet," Lady Salisbury said.

"Indeed. That is a great comfort to me," Violet said, rubbing her hands.

The bride entered on the arm of her father, followed by Catherine in a flouncy dress of cornflower blue and a ruched bonnet with a long yellow ribbon draped down her spine.

Scarlett's tiny frame was overpowered by reams of ivory organdie, satin and chiffon as well as the lamps burning bright upon her. She shrunk away from the eyes of Stanton Moore, her fingers tightening around the bouquet she carried.

Despite these fears, the ceremony went well. Scarlett relaxed her shoulders until they came to the line, she dreaded the most, when the signal went out that it was time to kiss the bride. They positioned themselves for the kiss.

Scarlett glanced around at the scrutiny of her friends and family watching from the sidelines. Her eyes locked with those of Romone Martin, whom she'd once found so attractive, and she faulted.

As she recovered and approached Frank, staring at his lips, the narrow, square toe of her shoe caught in the satin puddle at the hem of her dress. Averting her gaze, she struggled to free herself.

Frank wondered if her actions were a ploy to avoid the uncomfortable moment when their lips would meet. He shuffled his hands for a resting place.

As Scarlett had succeeded in freeing her foot, they jerked towards each other, Frank settling his fingers around her waist.

Scarlett pressed her hands against his firm chest, finding a bed there. She tilted her head back.

Their eyes locked until they could see right into each other's soul.

Diverting their heads to opposite sides, they almost clashed until Scarlett changed direction at the last moment, their lips meeting instead.

A rush of excitement swept through Scarlett, tingling in her chest. Having never been kissed in that way before, it wasn't how she anticipated it would feel. His lips were warm and juicy, impossible to move away from, in their compelling intensity. The sweet, woody scent of his cologne drew her in. His firm skin was a welcome place to nestle her head.

For Frank, it wasn't like any kiss he'd experienced before. Indeed, it was a shaky start, but he'd made allowances for that. No, it was the captivating warmth of her lips that struck him then. Her skin was soft like a pillow. Her hair as sumptuous as petals. Her perfume reminiscent of a summer spent in the garden.

Their lips became more intense as they clung tighter to each other.

Scarlett had a new sense of longing for her husband.

Frank was in a dream that he didn't want to end. Scarlett's kiss, given to him in her purity, was the anecdote to his loneliness.

Their minds reluctantly drew back to their guests as applause broke out and they were pronounced as a married couple before them. They wrenched themselves apart with a gasp of air to face the crowd, the spell shattered, the dream dispersed.

They beamed as they sauntered down the aisle.

Outside the entrance, they passed under the wedding arch with flowers interwoven amongst the vines. The chirping of the birds seemed more melodious to them now.

The wedding breakfast was a spectacular affair held on the lawn at Buckley House overlooking the lake. A plum cake decorated with glazed fruit graced the table as a centerpiece.

Mr and Mrs Henson glowed with pride as their daughter made such an excellent match. They enjoyed the seeming envy of their nearest neighbours, and rival families. They were not alone in this, as Mr Lattimer also basked in the envy of many young men there. Romone's lips drooped, his eyes staring at his hands as he conversed with Scarlett's father.

Frank was aware he'd made an excellent conquest in winning the hand of the most handsome, and the most accomplished young lady in all Stanton Moore.

"Congratulations, Lattimer. She is exquisite," the Earl of Simms said as he and Frank watched Scarlett from across the lawn in conversation with Catherine.

"Why, thank you. I know how lucky I am," Frank replied with a grin.

"You will be heading to Italy for your wedding tour, I understand?" the earl said.

"Yes, tomorrow. We will spend the night at The Gorge Hotel."

"Ah, The Gorge is magnificent!"

Meanwhile, from across the lawn, Scarlett said, "I'm well, Catherine. Don't you fret. Italy will be an excellent experience for me. Naima, my maid, will be joining me."

"You will have a familiar face, then? That's good. You will promise to write to me often?"

"Of course, Catherine."

"I know he will not influence you to be proud like he is."

"How could he?"

Catherine's gaze trailed across the lawn to Violet Ellingham. "His aunt is looking at me rather strangely. I fear she can read my lips."

"I think that is meant for me. At least we won't see her often at Closings," Scarlett said, following her gaze.

"I suppose that's some comfort," Catherine said, laughing.

Scarlett laughed too despite her misgivings from within.

It was late in the afternoon when the married couple eventually made their farewells, and they were finally settled in Mr Lattimer's carriage outside Buckley House that was ready to take them to the hotel.

The sun had just begun to wane with a promise of an excellent sunset that evening.

Mr and Mrs Lattimer waved to the guests as the carriage rolled away.

"WOULD YOU LIKE ME TO dress you now, Miss Scarlett?" Naima asked, patting dry her mistress' shoulders. The constant heat made frequent bathing a must.

Mr and Mrs Lattimer were in the middle of their wedding tour in the Italian Lakes.

Scarlett had breakfast in her nightgown on the balcony of her chamber. The villa itself was situated with a view of Lake Garda, which was breath-taking with the crystal blue water and mountain range towering above the lakes with a lush greenery reminding Scarlett of home.

"Yes, you may dress me, Naima, though I was enjoying the view immensely."

"Just so, madam. Who would not approve?"

"It is odd, though..." Scarlett said.

"What is?" Naima asked.

"You and I are in this room like it was old times again, and you're calling me madam. I cannot get used to it," Scarlett said as she stepped into a peacock blue carriage dress that Naima held open for her. She spun around with her arms held out as Naima fastened the buckle around the low waist of the dress.

"True, but the master would not like it if I neglected to call you by your proper title," Naima said.

"No, he would not."

"I think he is right, though. It would be unprofessional of me not to," Naima said.

"Of course not, Naima. Mr Lattimer likes his propriety. I cannot fault him for that." She sighed. "However, when we are alone, I'm sure it will be acceptable for us to continue in the old terms."

Naima nodded, then hesitated, as though willing herself to speak. "He treats you well, though? If I may ask? It's only out of concern for you that I do, as a lady's maid, and not as a nosy old busybody."

"I know you're not a gossip, Naima. Nor are you old. I'm acquainted with you well enough to know that, and I'm not offended that you should ask it. He treats me well enough."

"I'm glad about it, Miss Scarlett."

"It's still not ideal, though, is it? Marriages of convenience are never so," Scarlett said.

"No, Miss Scarlett, but your temperament is to make the best of situations. I see you have done that. I love you for it."

"Thank you, Naima. That means a lot to me," Scarlett said, embracing her.

The reality was that her marriage had not turned out the way she'd expected it to. Since their return from the hotel, Frank had grown more distant and secretive. The teamwork and influence she had hoped for were fast becoming a one-sided affair.

Upon her arrival in the hallway downstairs, she bumped into Lemuel, the butler at the villa. He was Italian born with jet-black hair greased to his skull. His moustache curled up at the edges. He had a kind face and very pleasant manners.

"Mr Lattimer said to inform you that he has gone out, Signora Lattimer. He won't return until this evening," he said.

"Thank you, Lemuel," she replied.

He bowed his head in kind acknowledgement of her gratitude, a rarity in his experience of dealing with Frank Lattimer.

She took a walk on the grounds to admire the vineyard as well as the view of the purple hills on the horizon. The warmth of the sun on her skin cheered her up, and she could feel herself tanning. She no longer cared that a golden tan was considered like a blemish instead of the milk-white skin that was so popular. She had a husband now, so what did it matter?

She headed for the lake path with a sketching pad. The parasol she held sheltered her head from the beating sun when sitting still. She poised her pencil to begin drawing the landscape. She adored the new trend of Romanticism because she loved to express herself with nature.

A picnic basket of lunch was brought out to her there and she savoured the salty taste of fish paste spread thickly on a crust of Italy's first-rate ciabatta. She tried a slice of pie, enjoying how the tangy apples sat nicely against the pork on her palate. Fishing in the basket for dessert, she found a fruit scone with a clotted cream and blackberry preserve accompaniment. All this she washed down with a glass of the finest port wine in the country, probably made from the fruit of the very same vineyard she'd seen earlier.

As she packed her things away, and headed back to the villa, she wondered what business could have taken her husband away so urgently that he should miss this lovely day.

CHAPTER ELEVEN

Mr Lattimer arrived back at the villa as dinner was about to be served, and Scarlett awaited him there at the table.

"Forgive me my tardiness. I had urgent business to attend to, and it kept me longer than expected," he said gravely, as he took his place. He didn't enlighten her further, and although Scarlett wanted to ask where he had been, she dared not risk her husband's displeasure by inquiring.

"I can bear the quietude well enough," she said, her face contorting.

"I'm sure that you can, darling. My money is a sufficient company for you, I have no doubt."

She shrunk away from him, studying his face to see if he would give anything away there. Finding none, she continued to eat the salad starter in silence.

"What you ladies find to do with yourselves is a mystery," he said, tucking a napkin into his shirt.

"I imagine so, to you," Scarlett said.

"Nor do I care to find out," Frank said.

"I expect not. I'm sure gentlemen are too busy with their secret business to care about us womenfolk."

His jaw froze.

As his eyes flashed, she wished the comment unsaid, knowing she would have to pay for it in strained silences.

He cleared his throat. "We will not discuss this further. I will hear no more of it."

THE NEXT MORNING SCARLETT'S unease was increased by seeing a strange visitor arriving unexpectedly from her bedroom window as she composed letters to Catherine and her mama. His weaselly facial features of a pointed nose and a short neck did nothing to ease her mind. He had a wide frame, and he wore an oversized suit as if to make him appear slimmer.

She calculated an hour had passed before he reappeared again.

I do not like the look of him.

She waited for him to be safely out of the way before she wrapped her shawl around her shoulders, taking out the letters as an excuse for a walk.

In such a gloriously romantic country like Italy it was hard for her to imagine why Frank had grown so distant. After their initial kiss, she'd begun to sense a deep attachment to her new husband. Why had his iciness returned?

Mr Lattimer stayed out of her way as much as possible for the rest of the wedding tour, and he spoke very little when in her presence. She found relief in the solitude.

He did not mention his visitor or the reason for his visit. She either had to continue to guess or put it out of her mind. She opted for the latter option.

SERENGETI'S VISIT HAD made Frank very uneasy, and, unfortunately for his new wife, it showed in his sharp outbursts of anger and low spirits.

"Just tell me, you fool," Frank said, his fists hitting the desk where the Italian sat.

Serengeti's small, pointed features never wavered. His chalk skin remained unmoved. Those beady eyes were steady to the last.

Frank pressed his lips together in irritation at the man's quiet calm. But to him, Serengeti had been a lifesaver. Despite his finding the man creepy and eccentric, his law skills couldn't be faulted. His input had been especially valuable in legal matters.

"You'll find it's all in order," Serengeti said, shuffling some papers. "All we need is your wife's signature, willingly or unwillingly."

Frank trembled. "I'll leave her to you. She'll trust a secretary."

SCARLETT WAS NO MORE relieved when the carriage arrived after a month to convey them to Closings, for she did not know what awaited her there. Her husband neglected to show her his estate before the wedding. The journey home was long and tedious and extremely hot, and her husband was not in a good mood, to add to the discomfort.

"Will I find Closings a pleasant place, Frank?" she asked, trying to ease the tension she was feeling, though his reply did not achieve this.

"I expect so. It is as it is," he said.

"Are the staff agreeable?"

"I suppose they are."

It seems I will have to wait and see then; she mused before settling down to sleep.

The road seemed to go on for an eternity, but when the carriage finally pulled up, the castle was awash with flames with servants running about the estate.

A voice cried out, "It's all going up this time!"

FRANK LISTENED TO SCARLETT'S breathing as he watched her sleeping next to him. He reflected on the wedding. The ceremony had been the easy part for him. He watched her lips now. He had braced himself for their first kiss, the only proper contact they'd had since his proposal, and she didn't disappoint him.

His problems started when they arrived in Italy. He hadn't meant to be withdrawn, but the turmoil in his mind was ready to blow. Not only that, but he also acted in the only way he knew how to under the strain.

His face contorted when he noted Scarlett's distress. If only he could mend it. The memory of his final hurried words with his aunt only added to his unease.

"Keep it to the last," Violet whispered in his ear before he boarded the carriage.

He shrugged. "What choice do I have?"

"I'll keep Closings safe until you return," she said, kissing a locket around her neck that was hidden beneath her buttoned collar.

THE CARRIAGE LURCHING forwards woke Scarlett with a start.

She gasped.

"It was only a bump in the road," Mr Lattimer said, who had perused a book.

"What hour is it?" she asked.

He took out his pocket watch, studying it closely. "It is precisely four in the morning."

She had slept through the night, then. All the anxiety must have made her weary. She slid back down in her seat, knowing with apprehension that there was still a way to go before they reached Closings. She wondered what awaited her when they got there.

"What is the matter? Are you so eager to become the mistress of Closings?" Frank asked.

"The journey is rather tedious, that's all." She frowned and turned her head to face him.

"You can't wait to get your hands on my money, eh?" he said, laughing.

"Why must you always talk of money?" she asked.

"Why? Because that is all that satisfies you about me, isn't it, my dear?"

"If you say so."

THE CLOSINGS ESTATE was very large containing ample variety of ground. The castle itself didn't come into sight until the carriage had conveyed them through acres of woodland, finally clattering into Closings courtyard as the sun was going down and the sky became grey.

Scarlett drew in a breath as she leaned out of the window and waited for her first view of the castle in the flesh. The anticipation vexed her until, eventually, there it stood before her.

Its impressively beautiful tower was like the prow of a ship sailing between rivers and looming out of the dimness. She called to mind the fairy tale palaces from her governess' stories.

The beige stones illuminated their path.

"So, this, my dear, is Closings," Mr Lattimer said as he handed her down from the carriage.

Scarlett gazed up at its walls. Her eyes filled with tears as the atmosphere of the estate welled up inside of her. There was a marked difference in the way the building was cast in shadow. How different it looked from the photograph. "You didn't tell me how grand it was."

On closer inspection, the reason for the shadows became apparent as some walls of the castle gave a scorched-like appearance, but underneath you could make out the same clean stonework that had once constituted those walls.

The servants, led by the butler and the housekeeper, formed two lines outside the entrance.

The butler, who was introduced as Larsson, bowed stiffly, his broad shoulders leaning towards her. His grey eyes seemed to hold some resentment there, yet she did not know if this had been imagined as he was a stranger to her.

Mrs Radcliffe, the housekeeper, was introduced next. She was a small person, about five and sixty, and her shining eyes stared impenetrably. Locks of sultry hair were styled away from her face and covered by a housekeeper's cap. "Welcome, Madam Lattimer," she said in a firm, crisp voice.

A plump woman with carrot hair and a blotched face, standing next to Mrs Radcliffe, was unmistakably the cook in a basic long dress and apron. She was introduced as Mrs Philips.

When all the staff had been introduced, Scarlett and Naima followed Mrs Radcliffe into the house to be shown to her chamber.

As they stepped inside, the stone courtyard was bare and oppressive until they passed through a low entrance where the room opened out with a fire blazing in the hearth. As they passed a set of steps leading below stairs, the constant hubbub welcomed them as the kitchen staff resumed their work. The hue of a musty stillness tinged with iron like smoking wood left Scarlett wondering how she would stand to be so often within these walls.

Mrs Radcliffe mounted the stairs and motioned for them to follow. The stairway was very dark, only emitting a square of light through the ceiling. When they reached the third floor they were led out onto a low-lit corridor. The walls were tall and covered with family portraits that Scarlett paused to observe. How strange it was that her husband's portrait was not amongst them.

"Your bedroom and boudoir are to the left, joined with the masters. You'll find it is very light and airy with an excellent view of the grounds," Mrs Radcliffe said as she swung open a door in the middle of the corridor and motioned for them to step inside. "Here we are, madam," Mrs Radcliffe said as they looked about the room.

A warm, yellow glow welcomed her, the bed being statelier than a canyon. She could grow to like this room.

"I hope you approve?" Mrs Radcliffe asked. Scarlett detected a hint of irony in her tone.

"Very much," she replied.

"I will leave you to change for dinner. Larsson will ring the gong when it is served," the housekeeper said.

"Oh, but Mrs Radcliffe, could you arrange for a tray to be brought up for me, please? I am rather tired from the journey," Scarlett said, stopping Mrs Radcliffe in her tracks.

"Of course, you may, madam." The housekeeper's jaw jutted out as she was speaking.

As soon as Mrs Radcliffe had left, Naima leaned close to her mistress and whispered, "I wouldn't want to get on her wrong side."

"I fear she was rather annoyed with me about dinner. I'm not sure if I imagine it, but I feel there is some resentment towards me amongst the servants," Scarlett said.

"I expect they're just as nervous as you are, madam. They will soon settle down when they see there is no harm in you. I remember being nervous myself when I first came to you at Buckley House. I confess, now don't be offended, I expected to find you a brat, but instead, I found a flower."

"Naima. Do you mean that?" Scarlett's eyes widened in amusement.

"I certainly do. They will come to appreciate you as I do. You'll see."

"I do hope you're right, Naima. What would I do without you?" Scarlett squeezed Naima's hand.

"I'm glad to be here to support you," Naima said, wiping away the tears that stung her eyes.

"I wish Catherine were here too."

"She can visit," Naima said, starting to unpack gowns from the first trunk.

"I hope so," Scarlett said, helping Naima.

"You shouldn't be helping me."

"I need something to do, Naima. It'll keep me steady," Scarlett said.

"I'll finish this," Naima said, snatching a garment from her mistress' hands.

Scarlett opted for a seat by the window and peered out onto the lawn, which was just visible by the light of the moon.

"Don't you worry yourself. It will turn out well. You'll see," Naima said, noticing her creased brow.

"Isn't that what you always say, Naima?"

"Yes, because it's usually true."

"Well, it wasn't true in the case of my marriage, but I hope you're right this time," Scarlett said.

"It may turn out to be a blessing in disguise yet," Naima said.

"I doubt that," Scarlett said.

"MAY I HAVE A WORD, sir?" Mrs Radcliffe said, entering the master's study to the rear of the castle.

"What is it?" he asked from his desk, setting aside the letters he had been perusing before she knocked.

"I am sorry to disturb you, sir, but I want to make you aware that madam has asked for a tray to be sent up for dinner this evening. I find this most inconvenient, sir, as a tray will already be sent up at breakfast. I cannot have my staff overworked. I would prefer it if she would dine downstairs in the evenings in the future."

"What reason does she give?" Lattimer said, running a hand across his face that was already haggard from the journey.

"She said she is tired from the journey, sir."

"That's fair enough for this evening. Should you not discuss the matter with her? She's the mistress now, you know? Household rules are always down to the lady of the house," Frank said.

"I would prefer it if you would mention this to her, sir. I fear I may appear to be overstepping my place."

"Very well. I will speak to her about it myself," Frank said.

CHAPTER TWELVE

"Naima, will you leave us for a moment?" Mr Lattimer said as he barged into Scarlett's boudoir the following morning. His hair was dishevelled, and his shirt was unbuttoned as though he had slept in his clothes.

Naima stood at the dressing table, brushing Scarlett's hair. She bowed promptly and left the room.

"What is the matter, Frank?" Scarlett asked, her eyes wide with fear at his wild appearance.

"Mrs Radcliffe has asked me to speak to you on the matter of mealtimes. She would like it if you would appear in the dining room in the future, apart from at breakfast, of course. I also join her in this wish as I don't want the servants' tongues wagging. Do you understand me?"

"That goes without saying. Mrs Radcliffe is against me in this too, I see. Am I to be commanded by a servant as well as by my husband? However, as I'd not planned on dining in my room in future, it doesn't matter."

"That must be sufficient. It is decided. I'm in no humour to argue about domestic matters, that is the mistress' prerogative. From now on you will discuss any such matters with Mrs Radcliffe."

"Then why did she not come to me and tell me?"

"I'll leave you to deal with her as you see fit. Good morning."

The door closed.

"Because Mrs Radcliffe is a coward, and she knows she's in the wrong," she answered for him. "We will have to see what Mrs Radcliffe says about that now, shan't we?"

"SHE SEEMS YOUNG, THE new mistress, doesn't she?" Sarah, the parlour maid, said in the kitchen.

"Yeah, how old do you reckon she is?" Fiona, the kitchen assistant, said, curling a loose strand of auburn hair around her finger.

"One and twenty, I believe," Mrs Philips chimed in over her shoulder as she kept an eye on the sauce she stirred for lunch.

"She seems stuck up, if you ask me. She has been used to her own way, she has," Sarah said.

"I'd say. I think she..." Fiona's voice trailed off when she caught sight of Naima.

They busied themselves with the chores as Naima sat at the solid oak table, mending one of Scarlett's dresses that had torn a sleeve.

"Is everything all right? Naima Patterson," Fiona asked, smirking.

"Of course, Fiona. Yourself?"

"I should say," Fiona replied.

"Were you discussing my mistress again?" Naima said, looking Fiona full in the face until she was forced to look away.

"We have been discussing her, yes. It is only natural," Sarah said.

"Yeah, we were just wondering how she's coping with the change and all, from one big house to another," Fiona said.

"It's none of our business to know, so be quiet, Fiona before Mrs Radcliffe or Larsson hears you. They won't stand for talking like this," Mrs Philips scolded.

"That old crow, Mrs Radcliffe. I don't like her," Fiona said.

"You wouldn't say it to her face," Mrs Philips said.

"You would listen to Mrs Philips if you knew what's good for you. I'll not pretend I didn't hear you two talking when I entered. I will not have my mistress run down; you hear me? You leave her alone, because not a sweeter heart ever breathed," Naima said.

"Spoken like a true lady's maid, Naima," Mrs Philips said.

"What is she doing with the master, if you think she's so good? Because he isn't sweet," Sarah said.

"I will not discuss it with you," Naima said.

"I was just wondering. This place is dreary," Sarah muttered, skulking to the exit, duster in hand. She stepped back as the door swung open.

Scarlett entered. "Oh, Sarah. Do you happen to know where I might find Mrs Radcliffe?" she asked.

"No, ma'am," Sarah said, blushing. She smoothed her blonde hair and the apron that covered her slim-cut figure.

"It doesn't matter. I'll find her," Scarlett said.

Sarah curtsied.

Scarlett had wandered through the house to no avail, searching for the housekeeper until she'd started climbing the spiral staircase, which led to the west wing of the castle.

A hand on her shoulder made her spin around. She came face to face with the woman herself.

The impenetrable gleam in Mrs Radcliffe's eyes intensified. Her jaw set firm as if in anger, yet when she spoke, her voice was steady and quiet. "Were you looking for me, madam?"

"Mrs Radcliffe, I believe there are some household matters to discuss," Scarlett said, still breathless from the recent shock.

Mrs Radcliffe froze. "Naturally, madam. The first matter I would like to make clear to you is that you must not go any further than these stairs in the future. This part of the house is forbidden. The master would be most displeased if he came to hear of anyone disobeying this rule," she said.

Scarlett stared. Maybe it had something to do with his parents' tragic deaths. Why would he be so guarded about that if it was common knowledge? There must be something else he wished to hide.

"Madam," Mrs Radcliffe said, bringing her back to the present. She realised she was still poised on the forbidden stairs.

She was grabbed firmly by the shoulders and pulled back into the corridor. The housekeeper awaited her instructions.

"Come to the morning room," Scarlett whispered.

CHAPTER THIRTEEN

"Frank, could I speak with you for a moment?" Scarlett asked, entering her husband's study.

"Can't it wait? I'm rather tied up here," he asked.

"No," she said walking to the window to show that she would stand her ground and have her say.

"What is it?" he said, turning his chair to face her.

"It's Mrs Radcliffe."

"What about her? I know she can be difficult," he said.

"Difficult, do you call it? She enforces rules as though I were little more than a servant in her employment."

"My dear, she has been a housekeeper here for as long as I can remember. She is more familiar with Closings than anyone, so it is hardly surprising she feels in control. Things have always been done her way. That does not undermine your authority as the mistress."

"That is not what's troubling me."

"Then, what is?"

"It's difficult to explain," Scarlett said.

Frank's hands grew restless, and a frown appeared on his brow.

"It seems she is hiding something. Lady Salisbury seemed to think..." Scarlett began. She stopped, catching sight of his eyes darkening.

"Don't be alarmed, I. . ." she said.

"What do you know?" he asked, diving from his chair and pacing the floor.

Scarlett swallowed, her eyes darting. "What did I say wrong?" she asked, her voice shaking.

"What nonsense has Lady Salisbury been filling your head with? What talk have you heard about this place?"

"Nothing. I... Lady Salisbury was only conjecturing. She said Closings had been shut up rather hastily after the tragedy, that was all. People like to make things up, but I have never heard any more talk about it. I'm sorry, my imagination runs away with me sometimes," she said.

He continued pacing the room.

"It does seem rather mysterious that you forbid the west wing. Why is that?" she asked.

Still, he continued pacing, his hands in his pockets and his face growing wilder.

"What is going on, Frank?" she asked, touching his shoulder.

He stopped short. When he turned to face her again, his eyes were wild and his face haggard.

"Leave me. I need to be alone," he said hoarsely.

She rushed out of the room, her dress rustling.

There is a secret here, she thought as she climbed the stairs to her chamber.

Naima was already there when she entered, laying out her evening gown. "Ah, madam. There you are. It is time to dress for dinner."

"Very nice, Naima," Scarlett whispered, eyeing up the dress. She sat in the seat by the window. Her maid noticed her heightened colour.

"What is it? If I may ask? You look distressed," Naima said.

"Oh, it's nothing," Scarlett said, passing a hand across her face.

"That's not what I see when I look in your face," Naima said, concern creeping into her own expression. She moved to where Scarlett was sitting, placing an arm around her shoulders. This proved too much for Scarlett, and she gave in to the relief of tears.

"Oh. You can talk to me. You know you can," Naima said.

"There is a secret in this house," Scarlett whispered, drying her eyes.

"Now, why does that not surprise me? There is always a secret in these great estates."

"Hush, keep your voice down, Naima."

"Don't be silly," Naima teased.

"Frank is keeping something from me. You did not see him when I confronted him about forbidding use of the west wing."

"There's talk in the servants' hall about that. I expect it's only speculation, though," Naima said.

"Mrs Radcliffe said it is forbidden. She was rather fierce about it too," Scarlett said.

"Well, she likes to be frightening, doesn't she? The old crow. She's just trying to usurp you to get her own way," Naima said.

"Do you think I imagine things, Naima? Frank was very angry about it, almost wild."

"He is only having a bad day. It will all be all right."

Scarlett rolled her eyes as her maid uttered this familiar statement. "If you say so."

"Come on, we had best get you into your dress now," Naima said, holding open the gown.

Scarlett stepped into the dress in front of the mirror and watched as it took shape over her slender figure.

Mr Lattimer appeared to be his usual self at dinner, and no more mention was made of their earlier conversation.

Afterwards, while they were settled in the drawing room, Larsson appeared.

"Excuse me, sir, but your secretary is waiting in your study," Larsson said.

"All right, Larsson," Frank replied. "Excuse me, my dear."

SCARLETT HAD MOVED to the pianoforte in the music room. She was in the middle of a sombre sonata to match her mood when Larsson entered, coughing loudly from behind her.

"Yes, Larsson?" she asked, turning to the door.

"I beg your pardon, but Mr Lattimer has asked for your presence in his study."

"Thank you, Larsson."

She paused at the door to the study, hearing voices within. Mr Lattimer was in conversation with a foreign accented gentleman who she presumed to be his secretary. She knocked gently, and he opened the door promptly.

"There you are, darling. Come in," Frank said.

When she entered the study, she was taken aback as she recognised the gentleman she'd seen at the villa leering at her.

"This is my secretary, Mr Serengeti," Mr Lattimer said.

The Italian smiled sinisterly as she approached him, and brushed her hand with his lips, rather too lingeringly, she felt. He gazed at her admiringly for what seemed like a long time. She crinkled her nose.

"Charmed, my dear Signora Lattimer," he said.

"Shall we get down to business?" Mr Lattimer said, annoyed by the prolonged attention the secretary was giving his wife.

"Absolutely, Lattimer," he replied, unwillingly letting go of Scarlett's hand.

Scarlett took the seat Mr Serengeti offered to her, and he leaned over her to open the document lying on the desk.

Her husband was studying the view of the grounds, reminiscent of Italy.

"Here we are," Mr Serengeti said, finding the last page of the document.

"Signora, I would like your signature right here," he said, resting his hand upon the biggest section of the paper, but leaving the signature box exposed. It was clear he wished to obscure part of the document from her view.

"I can't sign it unless I know what it contains," she protested, more to her husband than to Serengeti.

Frank ignored her, continuing to stare ahead in a daze.

"You would not understand, Signora," Serengeti said.

"My father taught me never to sign a document until I have first become familiar with its contents in full," Scarlett said.

A long pause followed where Scarlett pinched the bridge of her nose.

"My secretary is right, Scarlett. You would not understand it," her husband said, pivoting. He tapped his foot, flexing his fingers.

"Can't you at least give me an explanation of what it's pertaining to?" she appealed to him.

Frank's jaw tightened as he said, "I cannot. You must sign it."

Mr Serengeti signed for him to calm himself and said, softening his tone, "My dear Signora. You must sign."

"Why must I? I will if you will let me read it!"

Mr Lattimer ran a hand swiftly across his throat to put an end to the discussion. "We will leave it for the present."

Scarlett returned to the drawing room in a state of agitation.

An hour later, Frank joined her.

"I couldn't sign it, Frank. I hope you can understand," she said.

Frank strolled to the drink's cabinet, pouring himself a brandy.

Scarlett stared after him.

"I understand, of course. Business matters are just too long and drawn out. We need to get matters settled quickly," he said without turning around. He threw the contents of the glass down his throat and wiped his mouth with the palm of his hand.

Scarlett came to stand behind him. "You promised we would work together after I married you. Can't you keep your promise?" she asked.

He hesitated, then turned his head. Their lips almost touched. For a glorious moment his softened expression seemed to hint he would return to the Frank of their wedding. It was his eyes that changed first with a flicker of resentment in them, and he pulled away. "I must go. Serengeti is waiting for me."

She watched him leave with bitter disappointment gnawing away at her.

Mr Lattimer accompanied his secretary to London in the carriage, leaving Scarlett with a heavy feeling of unease.

Once again, sleep didn't come easily to her that night and she attempted to lull herself to sleep by taking turns about the room. When this didn't work, she flung open the balcony doors, and stepped out into the cool night air.

She had not stood there for ten minutes when she heard the distant clatter of a carriage. It roared towards the castle in a hurried motion. Moments later, it pulled up outside.

A gasp escaped her as Travers alighted, and with him her husband, who was helped down from the steps. He was led limping to the back entrance, clinging to his servant's neck.

Moving swiftly, she stepped into her chamber, carefully closed the doors to the balcony, and threw a patterned robe over her chemise nightgown, tying the drawstring waist around her.

She stole noiselessly to the kitchen where Travers had lit a fire. When she saw her husband, struggling to contain the blood that flowed from a cut on his forehead, looking as dejected as she'd seen him on the Simm's estate, she ran to his side.

"You're awake," Frank said from his place by the fire.

"Travers, what happened?" Scarlett asked, looking eagerly into his face.

"Our carriage was overturned on the road. Some darn bandits. Nothing was taken. I scared them away," Travers said.

Determined to nurse him, Scarlett tried to look at the wound.

Frank winced, moving away.

"I must insist. It's a nasty gash," she said, holding him steady. She ordered Travers to fetch her some hot water and a towel. After they were brought in, she asked him to send for the doctor.

"I don't need *his* help," Frank said.

"You do, Frank. There could be unseen damage," Scarlett said, dipping the edge of a towel into the now tepid water.

Closing his eyes, Frank allowed her to clean the wound, still wincing in pain every so often, but trying hard not to show how much he suffered. In truth, he enjoyed the closeness of her proximity even through the pain, and he enjoyed her seeming caresses. He cursed the interruption of the doctor and spoke sharply to him as he examined the damage.

Taking Scarlett aside, Doctor Baker pronounced his verdict in whispers.

"Why all this secrecy? Tell me, am I fit to travel, Doctor?" Frank asked desperately.

"I don't see why not. The wound is not as deep as it looks," the doctor said, picking up his medical bag. "As for your leg. . . that's another story."

"Ah, that's nothing," Frank replied, shuffling his leg out of sight.

"Then, I'll leave it up to you," the doctor said. With a smile to Scarlett, he left.

"You're not thinking of going to London?" Scarlett asked, opening the refrigerator door to see if Mrs Philips had any leftover food in stock. "There's nothing to eat," she said, biting her fingernail.

"Never mind. You retire. Travers will make up a bed down here for me, and I'll travel to London before you are up."

"Must you?" she asked anxiously.

"My aunt's expecting me," he said.

"We will eat first. You seem pale," she said.

"What is there?"

"I'll make us something."

"You?" he said, his eyes widening.

Scarlett smiled. "I can make an omelette. I saw Cook do it once at... home..." Her face fell and her voice faltered at the mention of Buckley House as it was a reminder of some happy times she'd spent with her father as they explored the globes in his office.

Frank, noticing the change, winced. "Come, come," he said, his voice cracking.

Scarlett noted his changed tone, and she saw it with pleasure.

"Make it if you must, but I'm sure you won't put Mrs Philips out of employment," Frank said.

She bent to kiss his hair, he submitted with a frown at her fussing.

She bustled to get the various pots and pans ready for the undertaking.

She whipped up the eggs with delight at her newfound skill and the omelette was ready in no time. Happily tripping around the table, she set out the plates and helped Frank to a chair.

"Well, this is a first," he said, offering a faint smile.

Scarlett laughed and Frank ate his first mouthful, chewing it thoughtfully.

Scarlett waited for his reaction, a knife and fork poised tentatively above her plate.

"That's not bad for a first attempt," he said to her relief.

Scarlett relaxed, and they ate in silence for a while.

"No one knows this, but I used to eat in the kitchen as a child sometimes," Frank said, breaking the silence.

Scarlett trained her wide eyes to gaze at his face. His voice had sounded different, less constrained, somehow. Her curiosity was piqued. "Me too," she said.

He gazed about the room. "I would steal baked goods when Cook wasn't watching."

"I stole some of Cook's pies," Scarlett said.

He stared. "You astonish me."

"We all have our moments," she said.

"Yes, we like to risk everything for the thrill of it. Take carriage riding, for instance," Frank said.

"Did you tell Travers to ride faster?"

"I was in a hurry," he said hoarsely, averting his eyes.

"Why the rush?"

He lowered his knife and fork, having left half of the omelette, and wiped his mouth on a napkin. When he spoke again, it was not in anger. He eyed her playfully and said, "That would be telling, and secrets are what make us interesting. Wouldn't you agree?" He got up and stole from the kitchen before she could make a reply.

How long she sat there after he'd left, she couldn't tell, but confusion was firm in her breast as she tried to piece together what her feelings really were for this man, this stranger who had so fast become her husband.

CHAPTER FOURTEEN

The following morning brought with it some guests from Stanton Moore to pay their respects to the bride. Mr and Mrs Henson arrived with Lady Salisbury and Catherine Kettering. They each embraced Scarlett as they entered the parlour, and Sarah brought in tea along with a selection of delicious cakes.

Despite how her pulse quickened with wondering what the arrival of Violet Ellingham would bring, and if her husband would manage the journey after his accident, Scarlett had to keep up a show of cheerfulness for her guests.

"How do you like being the mistress of such an outstanding castle, my dear?" Lady Salisbury said, a madeira sponge poised to her lips.

"Yes, it suits her very well. Can't you see how well she looks?" Mrs Henson said.

Lady Salisbury gazed at Scarlett. "Yes, it suits her very well." Her eyes turned to the tall, dark green walls of the drawing room and the large, square portraits surrounding them. "I've never seen Closings looking so elegant, either. But it can't be easy to take on, despite its glory. I hope you're not tiring yourself out," she said.

"I'm managing well enough. I thank you for your concern. Violet has been very helpful," Scarlett said, though the faintness in her voice showed otherwise.

Lady Salisbury clapped her hands. "Ah, dear Violet. She was always the practical one." She sighed.

"Mr Lattimer is out, so Larsson informed us," Mr Henson said after watching this badgering of his child with some pain and a sympathetic glance.

"He has gone to London to see his aunt, and she will come back to Closings with him for an extended visit," Scarlett said.

"How was Italy, Scarlett?" Catherine asked, toying with her hands.

"It's a magnificent country, Catherine. I hope one day you will get the chance to see it for yourself," Scarlett said.

"Oh, I would like that very much," Catherine said, her coffee-coloured eyes eager.

"Well, Catherine, your mama must get a move on with finding a rich gentleman for you to marry," Mrs Henson said.

Scarlett rolled her eyes and Catherine nodded sadly.

A little later, Catherine accompanied Scarlett on a tour of the castle grounds, letting her see some of her favourite places to retreat to when she needed a quiet moment.

"You must not mind what Mama says, Catherine. You know how she is? Your mama and mine have always been rivals," Scarlett told her once they were alone.

They headed towards the shimmering azure lake at the rear of the estate, while the rest of the party took a tour around the castle with Mrs Radcliffe.

"Don't worry, Scarlett. I know how mamas can be. I'm sad, though, that we cannot choose for ourselves. Likewise, I would so much like to marry for love, not money."

"I am a sad reminder that a marriage of convenience is less than ideal. That is why I must have you promise me to do what you have resolved in your heart, Catherine."

"Are you not happy? Have you not fallen in love with Mr Lattimer, Scarlett? It does happen."

"Well . . . I'm working on it, but it is tough with Violet's influence, I'm afraid to say. I can admit to you that I'm far from content. It's about to get even worse when the aunt arrives this evening."

"Then I am sorry for you, Scarlett. I do hope that you will fall in love with him eventually."

"Frank doesn't really open about his true feelings. He's a difficult man to fall in love with, but thank you for hoping," Scarlett said.

"You're well, though, Scarlett, aren't you? He doesn't mistreat you?"

"Only in words, sometimes, but no, I have no worries about that."

"I am glad. Is Naima a comfort to you?" Catherine asked.

"Dear Naima. I would have gone out of my mind already had it not been for her," Scarlett said.

"I'm so glad she could come along, and it is a fine castle, that surely is a comfort."

"It is an excellent castle, Catherine, and the solitude is most refreshing. I often come and sit here by the lake with my easel or sketchbook," Scarlett said, seating herself in her favourite spot under the tall cedar tree.

"It is a beautiful spot. I can see why you like it so much," Catherine said, leaning on her elbow under the tree beside Scarlett as she surveyed the fifteen acres of landscaped greenery that made up the gardens, reaching to the terrace with a view of the main lawn, and its range of beds and shrubberies.

The guests left mid-afternoon, leaving Scarlett just a few hours before Mr Lattimer arrived with his aunt. She ran to her chamber where Naima was busy sorting through Scarlett's old gowns to give to a poor family living in one of the cottages situated on the outskirts of the castle grounds. Scarlett had met the family while on her rounds when she took baskets of food to the poor community of Parsons Running. Upon learning the family had two daughters of fourteen and sixteen, she kindly offered the gowns.

"We have a few hours to take the gowns," Naima said, placing the clothes she had set aside in a trunk.

The manservant, Mr Travers, had agreed to take them in the carriage. He'd been sworn to secrecy, Scarlett not caring for her husband or his aunt to learn of the escapade. They could fully rely on his discretion as he did not care much for his master.

"We have time if we go now," Scarlett said, helping Naima close the trunk.

Mr Travers helped Naima carry the trunk to the carriage, and they got on their way.

Riding through the village, they passed the same spot where Scarlett's carriage had once mistakenly arrived. The deep sense of abandonment that had been present on that occasion returned and it only increased as she stepped down from the carriage outside the Farley's Cottage. None of the sounds you would expect to hear in a village met her ears.

There were several young children playing in the yard in rags. One of the young boys must have hurt himself as he was yelling and screaming as his mother hushed away the pain.

"What a sight to behold. Just like many families where I come from in Ireland. Such a shame," Naima lamented.

Mrs Farley caught sight of the carriage, and at once whisked the child away indoors, calling over her shoulder, "Shan't be a minute."

Mr Travers clambered down from the carriage and started to unload the trunk. He then helped Scarlett and Naima down from the carriage, and they squelched carefully through the mud to reach the clean porch. Naima helped Scarlett to hold up her skirts and petticoat. As they reached the cobbled yard, they smelt the damp air of washing on a line. Scarlett paused to consider how the inhabitants could exist in such cramped spaces.

"Begging your pardon, madam," Rosalie Farley said, appearing in the doorway, arms emptied of the child. "I had to get my Sammy a plaster."

"It is quite all right, Mrs Farley. Is the child recovered?" Scarlett asked kindly.

"He's just fine. Do step inside," Mrs Farley said.

They obeyed and were summoned to sit on wooden chairs in the cramped kitchen. A startled tabby cat ran across their path as they were about to sit, and they had to step aside to let it pass.

"Get away with you, Percy," Mrs Farley said.

She poured them all some tea and set the pot on the table.

Mr Travers entered, carrying the trunk and set it down in one corner.

"Thanking you kindly, sir," Mrs Farley said as he settled in a chair, and she passed him a cup.

"The pleasure is all mine, ma'am," Mr Travers said.

Naima wrestled to balance her cup as Percy returned and jumped on her knees.

"Shoo!" Mrs Farley said.

The cat turned around, giving her a cold glare before he settled on Naima's knee.

Naima stroked his head. "I don't mind cats."

Mrs Farley nodded and turned to Scarlett. "Thanking you for the gowns. My Lizzie and Sophie will be thrilled when they come home. That they will." She wiped her sweaty, mud-stained face with her sleeve. She smiled at Scarlett, showing a row of missing teeth. The hurt child came to settle on his mother's knees.

"I'm so glad I could be of use to you and your daughters in your time of need, Mrs Farley. I only wish I could help you more," Scarlett said, reaching across and placing a hand on her arm.

"You have done what you could, madam," Rosalie said, wiping away a tear with the back of her hand. "It's nice to find a kind heart up at the castle. It might be that you can melt some of the frosts that are settled in the village."

"The atmosphere here doesn't seem to have recovered after the fire," Scarlett said.

Mrs Farley clutched at her chest. "Oh, no. The tragedy of it still haunts you every time you go outside."

Scarlett held a hand over her heart. "I've felt that way too, Mrs Farley. I've wondered why Closings was shut up."

Rosalie planted a kiss on her little boy's head as he nestled in her lap. "Well, there was talk that the master, old Mr Lattimer, started the fire himself. He was a lunatic, they say. He wanted his wife out of the way." She rolled her eyes.

Scarlett clapped a hand to her mouth.

Mrs Farley eyed her with sympathy. "Don't fret, ma'am. I'm sure you're safe."

Naima coughed. "You forget yourself. Scarlett is the mistress now."

"I beg your pardon," Mrs Farley replied coldly.

Scarlett waved a hand to Naima. "You know I don't care about such nonsense."

Mrs Farley seemed to take her reproof as a sign to continue. "I'm sure it's all just a rumour, myself. Pay no heed to what I say."

Unfortunately for Scarlett, she couldn't heed this advice, and a new dread had settled in her chest as they rode home.

CHAPTER FIFTEEN

Violet Ellingham arrived with Mr Lattimer at precisely six o'clock in the evening.

Scarlett, who had changed into a low-waist evening gown with a large, embellished skirt, awaited their arrival in the drawing room.

Violet gave her the usual cold glare with her piercing dark eyes, and then kissed both sides of her face in turn. Mr Lattimer, fully recovered after the accident, went to change for dinner.

"I'm glad to see you, Mrs Ellingham," Scarlett said.

Violet offered no response.

Once Violet and her lady's maid had been shown to their rooms and had dressed for dinner, the dining got underway with a golden vegetable soup. They sipped the starter in silence. All they could hear was the clanging of spoons on porcelain. Mrs Ellingham looked very displeased with her nephew, leaving Scarlett wondering what had happened on their journey home.

Violet finally broke the silence on the second course. "This fish is not cooked quite right, it was never so before," she offered, a smug smile playing on her lips.

Her nephew put down his spoon and fiddled with the cuffs on his shirt. "It is the same as Mrs Philips always does it," he said.

"It cannot be," Violet said.

"You've not tasted it in a long while, perhaps your palette is weakening with age," her nephew jeered.

"I hope you're stamping your authority with the servants, Scarlett," Violet said, turning to her. "I have every faith in them, but they need a firm hand to show them the way."

"I may run the estate differently to you, but it's sufficient enough, I assure you," Scarlett replied.

"Really, Frank, she is quite peaky. Can such a creature really manage an estate as vast as this?" Violet asked.

Her nephew stared in front of him in silence.

"There is only one thing for it. I must offer my services more often, perhaps staying here for a while until things pick up a bit. What do you say to that?" Violet said, her lips curled into a half smile at her idea.

Scarlett opened her mouth to remonstrate, but Mr Lattimer spoke first. "I think it would not be good at all. You should mind your own business in future, Aunt. There is nothing wrong with the way things are run, and I will not have Scarlett criticised in this way."

Scarlett paused and looked up from her plate. She felt her colour heighten at this sudden turn of events.

"Frank, please. I'm only trying to help, you know I am. What do you say, Scarlett?" his aunt said.

"Thank you for your kind offer, Violet. I'm sure you mean well, but I would not like it at all," Scarlett said, politely, yet firmly.

"I will hear no more of this nonsense, Aunt Violet," Mr Lattimer said.

"How will she manage? I must be of assistance," Violet said.

Scarlett glanced uneasily at her husband. She had forgotten about the ball, and feared lest she could not cope with organising things.

He turned her way for a moment. As if reading her thoughts, he said, "Mrs Radcliffe can be of assistance. She has been here the longest."

"We will see now, won't we?" Violet hissed.

When the dinner was at an end, Violet joined her nephew in his study to talk with him privately. Scarlett waited in the drawing room alone, where, after the heat in the dining room, a welcome cool night breeze blew through an open window. She glanced out on the night for a moment, then picked up a book she had been reading earlier, leafing through the pages, her attention divided from thoughts of what was occurring in the study. An idea struck her, but she dismissed it with a wave of her hand, until the idea pushed itself forward in her mind again, and she gave way.

Why should I not know what is being said? It would not actually be eavesdropping as it is my business too. I am mistress here, she thought, as she slipped off her shoes. Leaving them by the sofa, she glided from the room, closing the door softly behind her.

She crept gingerly along the half-lit corridor as if she were breaking in while the household were asleep, and she stopped to listen before passing the stairs.

When she reached the study, she carefully placed an ear to the door and listened.

She could just make out the rustling of Violet's gown as she must have been pacing around. She heard her husband speak first.

"So, what do you suggest, exactly?" he asked.

"That you allow me to foresee all the arrangements for the ball. No one needs to know I am involved, apart from Mrs Radcliffe, and she will not mind. It is not her place to see to the arrangements."

"Why is it so important to you?" Frank asked.

"I cannot afford gossip being spread abroad because of mismanagement as we don't know what they might dig up in the process. We cannot have too much notice taken of our ways at Closings. The secret must not be exposed, under any circumstances, or we would be ruined," Violet said.

"It will not be," Frank said.

"Not if we are careful and we don't draw too much attention to ourselves. There must be no talk of the old ballroom. Any mention of it must be quashed."

"There shall not be. The new ballroom is grand enough and it is much better situated than the old one. No one will see anything is a-miss."

"Yet, they may wonder about the old one."

"Let them wonder. They will never guess the truth."

"Does Scarlett truly have no idea?"

The hairs on Scarlett's neck bristled when she heard her name mentioned, and a strong sense that she was being watched crept over her. Goosebumps prickled on her arms. She turned her head quickly, expecting to see Mrs Radcliffe lurking in the shadows, but the corridor was empty. She breathed easier as she carried on listening.

"There's no need to worry about my wife. She will not speak a word of her suspicions to anyone if she knows what's in her best interests," Lattimer said.

"Does she know, though? I doubt it. She is so young and headstrong," Violet said.

"She knows. Believe me."

"What about the document? Did you get her to sign it?"

"I'm afraid not," Frank said.

"Not even with the assistance of Serengeti? You, see? So headstrong, I knew it. She cannot be trusted at all. You must be careful what you tell her."

"She knows nothing beyond her own suspicions," Frank said.

"So, she does suspect?" Violet asked.

There was a pause in the conversation, during which time, Scarlett could hear her own heart beating. She also became aware of the sound of heavy footsteps coming up the stone steps. She had to think quickly.

It was too late to go back to the drawing-room now!

She had to find a place of concealment. She fumbled around the walls of the dark corner, looking for a nook or a crevice. Her hand brushed against what felt like a large picture frame. As her hand touched the left-hand corner, the frame swung open, and she stepped into a secret passageway.

The picture swung shut behind her, plunging her into complete darkness.

CHAPTER SIXTEEN

She waited, then heard a knock, then Larsson's voice at the study door. Once she had heard the door click shut again, she pushed frantically on the picture. She had to get back to the drawing-room before she was missed.

She pushed harder on the picture and fumbled for a handle, but it was of no use, for it would not budge.

A panicky, sickening feeling came over her.

There must be a way out.

She breathed deeply to calm herself down.

Carefully feeling her way along the walls, she moved slowly along the narrow passageway. After what seemed like an eternity, she came across a set of stone steps. She gasped as she felt a drop beneath her feet. She came to an abrupt stop. Cold air drifted upwards, bristling her hair like flowers in a storm. She flapped her arms to keep her balance.

Recovering herself quickly, she started to descend the extremely steep stairs.

Eventually reaching the bottom step, she was met with a sharp turn and had to cling to a jagged point in the wall to avoid falling on her face.

Then she came across another staircase, twisting around the corner. Below these stairs, was another long passageway.

She leaned against a wall to rest.

To her relief, she found a door in the wall. This passage led her to an old room that was thick with dust and cobwebs. She coughed as dust lodged in the back of her throat. The row of windows gave off a little light from the moon, revealing white sheets, covering articles of furniture. The once rich woodwork on the walls was full of burrowed woodworm. The floor of the balcony above had completely disintegrated. A four-tiered chandelier hanging low in the middle of the room had lost its sparkle. Bouncing on the floor with her bare feet, it was springy like a dance floor. She recalled the conversation she'd just overheard in the study.

The old ballroom, of course.

Spinning around in the centre of the floor, her dress splaying out at the sides, she imagined she was dancing at the famous ball. As she got nearer to the walls, she could just make out massive portraits hanging there, but she couldn't recognise any of the subjects.

This must be the Lattimer family.

Realising she had wasted too much time already, she made for the door. It was stiff, and she pulled it with all her strength, placing a foot on the wall beside it. As it eventually gave way, it swung open with a groan.

She came out onto another corridor, and to her relief, she did not meet Mrs Radcliffe. She ran along it, passing rows of closed doors and going down the spiral staircase that the housekeeper had earlier informed her led to the west wing.

So, it is a secret passageway to the west wing.

She rushed back to the familiar part of the castle and her breath came easier again as she was dashing back to the drawing room, pausing at the door to listen if voices came from within. Hearing nothing but silence, she went inside, slipped on her shoes, and picked up the book she had left lying open on the curved armrest of the sofa.

A WEEK AFTER THIS CLOSE encounter, the Lattimer's as well as Violet Ellingham were guests at Salisbury Manor. Scarlett had not quite recovered herself, and it showed in a quiet depression of spirits.

This was noted by Lady Salisbury with concern and mentioned occasionally throughout the dinner.

"Don't fuss, I hate it. Mama used to be like that," Scarlett said faintly.

"She only acts out of concern for your welfare, as I do. As you are so close to Buckley House, why don't you call? It might help to be at home again," Lady Salisbury said.

Violet put down the cutlery she used. "Are you hoping to be rid of us sooner than planned?" she asked, wiping at the corners of her mouth with a napkin where an amused smile threatened to break out.

"Not at all, Violet, but you must admit she looks quite pale," Lady Salisbury said.

"Can't we get on with our meal?" Scarlett pleaded.

"I won't say another word, but you really must get more rest," Lady Salisbury said.

"How about the estate for a more interesting topic?" Lord Salisbury said.

"Oh, you old bore. Can't you come up with something more engaging?" Lady Salisbury said.

"Well, someone must manage these things. To top matters off, my tenant farmer is leaving. You don't happen to know anyone who can fill the role?" He addressed his question to Frank.

"I can't help you, I'm afraid. Our tenant farmer is never heard of. He performs his duties very well," Frank replied.

"They're not like our servants," Lady Salisbury said, lifting a glass to her lips.

Scarlett's spirits diminished as the evening progressed, particularly when the conversation turned to the Closings annual ball.

"I remember the last ball we attended at Closings, don't you, my dear?" Lady Salisbury asked her husband.

"Indeed, I do," he replied, scraping his plate of every morsel.

"It was done with such elegance and graciousness. I'm sure Scarlett can pull that off too," Lady Salisbury continued.

"I'm not so confident she can," Violet said, looking sideways at her nephew, sitting beside her.

Before Mr Lattimer could see, Scarlett fainted on his shoulder. He caught her in his arms, swallowing constantly. "She must rest," he said, stroking her neck.

"I could see she was not well, poor thing," Lady Salisbury said, getting up quickly, and rushing to her aid.

"It must be the pressure of hosting the ball. I told you it was all too much for her, but would anyone listen?" Violet said.

As soon as Scarlett had recovered herself enough to walk, Lady Salisbury led her upstairs to one of the bedrooms so she could rest before their journey home.

"Are you sure you're not ailing, my dear?" Lady Salisbury asked Scarlett who was lying on the bed.

"I will be after I have rested a little," Scarlett replied, turning on her side.

"Are you perhaps with child?"

"No, I don't think so."

"It is perhaps the heat. It is rather stuffy tonight. I'll open a window and leave you to rest now," Lady Salisbury said.

The journey home that evening was a solemn one, each looking through the window of the carriage with their own silent reflections.

Violet glared straight ahead of her, thinking of the gossip that Lady Salisbury may spread because of Scarlett's lack of judgement.

When they reached Closings, Scarlett a-lighted hurriedly, just stopping long enough to thank Travers for handing her down from the carriage. He returned her gratitude with an anxious look.

As she ran upstairs, holding up her gown to keep from tripping, she overheard Violet telling her nephew that she wanted to speak with him in the drawing room over a brandy. Feeling an impulse to know what they were hiding, she waited on the stairs, hidden from view. She then softly descended them, stopping to listen behind the door, looking frequently over her shoulder in case any of the servants happened to be passing that way.

"Really, Frank, she had to make such a display of herself, and here was I, not wanting to draw attention to ourselves at this time," Violet lamented.

"I think she suspects something," Lattimer said warily.

"Nonsense, Frank. What can she possibly suspect? She knows nothing, as you said."

"I wouldn't be too sure of that, Aunt Violet. I believe she heard from Lady Salisbury that things were hasty when we left Closings."

"Lady Salisbury? What does she know? It is only conjecture, after all," Violet said.

"That is what my wife said," Frank said.

"I'm sure she cannot know a thing, as I said."

"She knows something is wrong," Frank said.

"What will you do?"

"I can hardly grasp an idea."

"Speak to her about it. Find out how much of the circumstances she's acquainted with," Violet said.

"How can I do that without telling her all?"

"Use tactful questions, perhaps?"

"She will suspect something if I start to ask her questions all of a sudden."

"Tell her all and swear her to secrecy," Violet said.

"Too risky. She may talk to get her revenge on me," Frank said, his tone downcast.

"Make something up then, that would be better than her finding out the truth. Just do something to allay her suspicions. You have been too guarded with her. Go to her now and inquire about her health," Violet said, her words growing more intense.

"Don't touch me. It's you who got me in this mess," Frank said.

"You owe me your life, Frank. Your very respectability depends on me. Don't you forget it," Violet said.

Scarlett did not wait to hear more as she suspected her husband was about to visit her room.

CHAPTER SEVENTEEN

Scarlett had been right, for just as Naima had helped her on with her night ensemble, there was a light knock on the door. Naima opened the door and stepped aside for Lattimer to enter.

"Will that be all, madam?" Naima asked.

"Yes, Naima. You may go now," Scarlett said as she draped a shawl around her shoulders.

"Forgive me if I disturb you, darling. I wanted to make sure you are recovered," he began softly. She could almost have believed he was sincere had she not overheard the conversation in the drawing room.

"I am as well as can be expected under the circumstances," she said casually.

"You're not ailing? I can send for Doctor Baker if you would like?" he asked.

"No, don't trouble yourself. I expect it was the heat. I'm well now, really."

"If you change your mind, just let me know."

The colour drained from Scarlett's face, and she struggled to keep her composure. She wanted to demand there and then that he tell her all. Instead, her eyes pierced his soul. "Why this sudden concern for my welfare? Because you do not care for me, do you, Frank?" she said, angling away from him. "You're the most selfish man I have ever known because you married me against my will." She was hardly aware that she had become hysterical and that she was frantically hitting him with her fists.

Frank gently took hold of her wrists, managing to get her to lie on her bed. He rushed out of the door and called for Naima, who appeared promptly.

"What is it, sir?" Naima asked, breathlessly.

"Can you go to your mistress? She needs consoling," Frank said.

Naima's eyes flashed before she replied, "Yes, sir."

Lattimer disappeared swiftly downstairs to join his aunt again in the drawing room. Naima calmed Scarlett, giving her a sleeping draught. She stole noiselessly from the room, muttering curses aimed at Mr Lattimer.

"THEY HAD A ROW LAST night, didn't they, Naima?" Sarah said in the morning as the servants were assembled at breakfast.

Larsson and Mrs Radcliffe had not yet arrived, and Mrs Philips still sweated over the stove, hardly noticing what was said in the background. This gave Sarah an opportunity to gossip.

The kitchen was a very practical room with everything to hand.

Naima wildly buttered a slice of bread. "I don't wish to discuss it with you, Sarah," she said.

"How do you know they had a row?" Fiona asked, leaning forward with interest.

James, the eldest footman, rolled his eyes. "I expect it's all lies, Fiona."

"It isn't. I heard it, I did," Sarah said, falling back in her chair. She folded her arms across her chest.

"When? We heard nothing," James said.

"When I was turning down the bed in the master's room," Sarah said.

"Was it? Sarah," Fiona asked.

"Yeah, properly screaming with hysterics she was," Sarah said.

"The mistress was, you mean?" Naima corrected.

"You know whom I mean," Sarah said.

"I can't say I'm surprised, mind you. It's enough to make one scream being married to that horrid man, though he is my master," Mr Travers said, who had been listening attentively at the other end of the table.

"You ought to be careful, Mr Travers. You don't want such talk to get back to the master," Naima said, her brow creased with concern.

Travers smiled at her in reply.

Mrs Radcliffe entered the kitchen, followed by Larsson, and there was a screeching of chairs as they all got to their feet.

"ARE YOU SURE YOU'RE quite fit for riding this morning?" Naima asked as she secured the buttons on Scarlett's peplum riding jacket, later that morning.

"I told you, Naima, I'm quite recovered," Scarlett said.

Naima's small fingers nimbly tied the neckerchief around Scarlett's neck. "As long as you're sure."

"I'm sorry, Naima. I must get away from here for a while," Scarlett said.

"You won't ride too far?"

"I'm meeting Catherine in Stanton Moore. She has some news for me, then I will visit with my mama and pa."

"Ah, it may be good for you to see them," Naima said, handing her a riding whip.

Scarlett headed for the door, her voluminous skirt swishing.

Percy, the white stallion her husband gave her as a wedding gift, was saddled and waiting for her when she reached the stables.

"Are you ready, Boy?" she asked, caressing his head before swinging herself up on the saddle.

She met Catherine at their favourite café in Stanton Moore. Before entering the café, she couldn't help taking a glance around the village. She found it hard to explain why the nape of her neck prickled as she did so. Shrugging, she went inside.

Many a curious glance was directed her way as people recognised the new and influential mistress of Closings. As she removed her veil and top hat, women whispered to each other about the latest riding fashions she adorned.

Catherine was very excited about the news of her new beau, a captain in the Militia by the name of Thomas Jepson. How they came to meet. How she had defied her mother who did not approve of the match. "Mama doesn't approve of the Militia, but I would have my way," Catherine said.

Scarlett couldn't hear this speech without some consternation. Why didn't she have the courage to be as defiant as her friend in the face of society?

"Good for you, Catherine. I'm so glad you are marrying a man whom you can respect," Scarlett said, eyeing up the tray of miniature cakes on the table.

"I do respect him with all my heart. Indeed, I do," Catherine said.

"I'm glad of it. I will look forward with eager anticipation to meeting him. Naturally, I'll see that you are both invited to the ball," Scarlett said, her tone taking on a note of sadness as she glanced out of the window at her old village, considering how much she preferred the hustle and bustle that she missed in the deserted Parsons Running.

Her mind flew back to when she was seventeen again and to when Catherine used to visit Buckley House. She remembered the lively discussions they'd had in the gardens about what they'd wanted to do with their lives when they came of age.

A hand on her arm brought her back to the present, and she turned to her friend apologetically.

Catherine's head tilted to the side. "Is everything all right? You seemed miles away."

Scarlett's hands instantly flew to her burning cheeks. "Did I?"

Catherine nodded. "There isn't any trouble, is there? You can tell me."

Scarlett shuffled. There seemed no need to burden Catherine with her suspicions, so she forced a smile and said, "I was remembering old times."

Catherine smiled. "Yes, we had some good times."

"If we could only go back," Scarlett murmured, but it was too low for Catherine to overhear, and her friend turned to the window with a huge grin of contentment on her face.

When they left the café together, the unease she'd felt on the way in, returned. Scarlett became aware of a man watching her closely while he leaned against the stone wall of the café, a bulldog at his heels. He chewed greedily at a piece of leftover pie. The man seemed to hang on every word Scarlett and Catherine uttered as they prepared to mount their horses.

Scarlett made haste to swing herself on her horse, pushing back her hair to replace her hat. She spied him out of the corner of her eye.

His apparel was threadbare, and he had a thornbush for a beard. His eyes gave a cross-eyed expression as they made contact. When he realised she had spotted him, he moved away, snarling at his dog to follow.

Had Violet sent her spies to follow her now?

She jerked the reins at every sudden sound or movement in the trees on the lonely road home.

CHAPTER EIGHTEEN

After she'd dropped off Percy at the stables, Scarlett met Mr Serengeti on his way out of the castle. It was too late to retreat out of his sight as she would have wished, and she had no choice but to allow herself to meet with this terrible Italian.

"Ah, Signora Lattimer. What a pleasure this is," he said, kissing the hand she unwillingly offered to him.

"Mr Serengeti," she said, shivering inwardly as his lips brushed her skin.

"You brighten my day, Signora. Such a beautiful form before me." He reached out to touch her face. She pulled away from him and ran into the castle, almost colliding with her husband in the hallway.

"What is the matter?" Frank asked, frowning when he saw her distressed expression.

"That man accosted me," she said with irritation.

"You mean, Serengeti?"

"Who else? I don't like him. Can you get rid of him?"

He laughed. "I'm afraid not. He is necessary to me, and to you too, for that matter, so you must be kind to him."

"Does kindness mean I should give in to his advances?" she asked.

"That is not what I meant. I will not allow him to compromise my wife. However, you must be as civil as possible to him," Frank said.

"If you wish," she said, glowering.

"Oh, Frank! Scarlett!" Violet said as she glided down the staircase ahead of them.

"Aunt Violet is about to leave for London," Lattimer said.

"Oh, I'm sorry," Scarlett said unconvincingly.

Violet narrowed her eyes as she stepped closer to her. "You look much better. I was concerned when I heard you had gone out riding, but the air has done you good, it seems."

"Yes, thank you," Scarlett said.

"Travers will be along directly," Mrs Radcliffe said, entering the hall.

"My trunks are all ready to be loaded onto the carriage," Violet said.

The days passed rather quietly at Closings after Violet's departure and Scarlett tried to put away the thoughts that had caused her such distress. This ease of mind was not likely to last. Mrs Radcliffe had compiled a list of the servants' duties to be carried out in preparation for the occasion in question. Scarlett left matters in the housekeeper's capable hands, though she was consulted to give her opinion of the arrangements.

"How are the plans coming on?" Lattimer asked over dinner.

"I thought household matters didn't interest you," Scarlett said, chewing on a piece of meat.

"I'm simply curious, that's all. I wouldn't want it to turn out to be a disaster. It is, after all, our first ball," Frank said.

"And I suppose society would frown upon it if it was anything less than perfect," Scarlett said.

"First, the opinion of society is certainly important in our game, yet I gather the very notion of society disgusts you, darling," he said.

"It is true that society, in general, must be satisfied, yet I take issue with many of its forms," she said.

"You should be careful, you are beginning to sound like a revolutionary," Frank said.

"My views don't go beyond these walls, so there is no need for anyone to hear about it," Scarlett said.

He pointed a finger at her. "But while you are behind these walls, I still expect you to behave as society sees fit. I will not allow my wife to make a fool of me," he said, his pitch gradually increased.

"Do I not behave so?" Scarlett asked.

"Not in all things."

"To what do you object?" she asked with trepidation lest he should list eavesdropping and snooping amongst her faults.

"The way you treat the servants, for instance. You're far too familiar with them, particularly with your lady's maid," he replied, refilling the green port glass.

"Now you sound like Mama."

"Maybe you should have listened to her more often. You cannot be too careful what you say to them. They are terrible for gossip, you know?"

"Naima has been with me a very long time. Naturally, I'm close to her. I can testify to her discretion," Scarlett said,

"I must insist that you speak to her and the other servants only when it is necessary to do so and that you never, under any circumstances, discuss the business of this house with them. If I ever hear that you have disobeyed me in this, I will see to it that your maid is put out of her position. No reputable household will ever employ her again," Frank said.

"You are now resorting to blackmail to keep me quiet. I do not understand why you think this is necessary. Naima hardly ever goes beyond these walls. She's not acquainted with anyone of consequence to communicate with in Parsons Running. What exactly are you afraid of, Frank?" she asked, looking him straight in the eyes. She noticed him flinch, avoiding her gaze.

"Just do as I say," he said, under his breath.

"What happened to the Frank I spoke to in the kitchen?" she asked.

"I'm not that man. You've dreamed him up. I'm more practical than I used to be."

LATER, WHEN SCARLETT entered the kitchen, Mrs Philips was covered in crimson blotches as she stood over a hot stove. Her hands stirred three separate pans. Fiona prepared a batter at the work surface, whisking with excellent wrist action. They paused in their work as she entered.

"I've come to speak with Mrs Radcliffe in her sitting room," Scarlett said quickly, to put them at their ease.

"By all means. Would you like some tea fetching?" Mrs Philips said in her jovial voice.

"No, thank you," Scarlett said.

The housekeeper's sitting room was located through a passageway leading from the kitchen. The door was ajar when she reached it, so she knocked lightly and entered.

Mrs Radcliffe frantically shuffled important-looking papers around in her desk drawer. She paused when she saw her mistress, stifling a cry. After a moment's hesitation, she hurried to sit at her desk. "Won't you take a seat?" Mrs Radcliffe said, peering above a pair of tiny spectacles.

Scarlett sat opposite her on a small chair under the window. "Have you lost something?" she asked tentatively.

The housekeeper waved a hand. "It's nothing urgent. Here is the plan of the ballroom. The decorations and such to get ready for the ball. Once you have looked it over, and approved the arrangements, or not, as you see fit, we will see what is to be done," she said, pushing the plans along the desk toward her.

"That all looks in order, Mrs Radcliffe," she said, after perusing the plans thoughtfully for a few moments. She dared not question the arrangements, or for that matter, anything Mrs Radcliffe did.

"That is grand. We shall get started on the preparations immediately," Mrs Radcliffe said.

There was a pause, during which time Mrs Radcliffe glared at her in expectation.

Scarlett hesitated and toyed with the frilly edge of her gown. "Mrs Radcliffe, may I ask you something?"

"Naturally, madam."

"Was the old ballroom as grand as the new one is?"

Mrs Radcliffe looked surprised and hesitated before replying. "How do you know about the old ballroom? Did the master tell you himself?"

"No, my friend Lady Salisbury used to attend gatherings here many years ago, and she recalls its existence," Scarlett said.

"Ah, I see. Yes, it was very grand and I myself have some very fond memories of it." Her voice trailed away. She looked to be in a dream for a few moments. "I was not sixteen when I came to Closings. Madam Isabella was a fine lady, very genteel and soft-hearted. A real beauty too," she continued with a smile, the first time Scarlett had ever seen her do so. "She whirled around that ballroom in true style, no mistake." Mrs Radcliffe's face darkened suddenly, and she shook her head until she became the same stern woman once again. "I would prefer not to discuss the details with you, however, as the master has not authorised me to do so."

"I see," Scarlett whispered, lowering her eyes.

"It is, alas! A very painful chapter in the master's life. That is why he does not wish it to be spoken of. He does not want to disturb the painful memories it evokes," the housekeeper said.

"I understand. I appreciate your honesty, Mrs Radcliffe."

"REDWOOD, MUST YOU DO your needlework here, I've got the dinner to lay out before it goes upstairs," Mrs Philips said sharply to the pert woman with pixie features and short, frizzy hair.

Margaret Redwood came with Violet Ellingham as her lady's maid. She was at the table plying her needle.

Scarlett had not long since quitted the servants' hall.

"Approach Mrs Ellingham about it if you dare," Redwood said quietly, refusing to move.

Mrs Philips opened her mouth to object, but she was interrupted by Mrs Radcliffe's unmistakable plodding step in the hall. All in the kitchen stopped what they were doing, staring at her with expectant faces as she entered and stood before them like a dark cloud.

"Some papers pertaining to this household are missing," Mrs Radcliffe said, eyeing all in the kitchen with a stern expression.

Redwood's tiny mouth set in a determined way as she continued to ply her needle on one of Violet's gowns.

Mrs Philips started to arrange the strips of pastry on the lattice pie, turfing the gown Redwood worked on to one side.

Sarah pretended not to hear as she was engaged in washing the dishes at the sink.

Naima kept her head bent over a book at one end of the servants' dining table.

"Well?" Mrs Radcliffe said.

"It's possible Signor Serengeti took them back to London with him," Redwood said.

"No. The paperwork never gets past me. The master would have asked for my permission," the housekeeper said.

"Wait, I saw you hovering around Mrs Radcliffe's sitting room last night," Sarah said clumsily, her arms up to the elbows in bubbles.

A smug smile played on Redwood's lips as she stared at her needle.

Mrs Philips' eyes narrowed.

Naima peered above the book with curiosity.

"My instructions come from Violet," Redwood said.

"You will refer to her as Mrs Ellingham," Mrs Radcliffe said, drawing herself up. "And I will ask her myself." Mrs Radcliffe stormed from the kitchen, closing the door firmly behind her.

THAT NIGHT, SCARLETT found sleep difficult as she anticipated tomorrow's events with extreme anxiety. Scenarios of events going horribly wrong played out in her mind. Visions of tearing her frock before she'd even made it downstairs came to mind, clumsy servants spilling champagne on guests as they delivered the glasses into their hands. She mulled through the dance moves in her mind, humming the tunes and counting, one, two, three every so often. What a laughingstock she would be if she simply put one foot wrong.

Stretching her arms above her head, she grappled with the pillows. She had to sit up. Forcing the pillows upward until they'd settled against the headboard, she slowly edged herself into a sitting position, using the pillows to cushion her back.

That's when she saw it.

An orange glow poured into the room through the gap beneath the door, and it seemed to hover there until it caught her eye briefly before it vanished again, plunging the room once more into blackness.

A sickening dread merged in her stomach as she realised someone had passed her room with a candle in hand, and with the history of fires at Closings, the circumstance did not bode well.

Reaching for her tea gown on the divan beside her, she slipped out of bed, planting her feet inside a pair of slippers and tiptoed to the door, cautiously turning the handle.

With a sharp bob of her head in both directions along the corridor, she could tell the coast was clear, but she could also make out the same orange glow to her left.

She crept from the room, following its leading.

CHAPTER NINETEEN

Scarlett awoke with a start at daybreak, on the morning of the ball. Her head spun as she tried to recall what she'd seen after following the candlelight signal. As she'd been getting lots of nightmares lately, she wondered if that had been a dream too.

As she struggled to move, a dull ache throbbed at the back of her neck, and she massaged it away. It hadn't been a dream. She remembered now. She'd been hit from behind. Who hit her? And why?

When she felt equal to moving, she sat by her window watching the sun rise over the lake and shimmer across the water as she tried to piece together exactly what she'd seen before everything went black.

A dark figure, that's what she'd seen.

Their face had been obscured by a hooded cloak, and they moved swiftly. Much too fast for Scarlett to keep up and get anywhere near them. Cradling her head in her hands, she tried desperately to recall what happened next.

It was all a blur.

Then, slowly, visions popped up in her mind.

The west wing.

The old ballroom.

Yes, she was led on a circular tour of the castle.

She recalled how the door groaned as it had done the first time, she'd used it.

"Mrs Radcliffe," she murmured.

It had to be the housekeeper as they had been talking about it a few hours before in her study.

Her mind flashing back once more, she remembered the door had closed in her face and she'd crouched down at the keyhole to watch the proceedings.

She groaned, trying to think what she saw within.

That's all she remembered.

Mrs Radcliffe must have extinguished the candle and hid in the shadows after allowing the door to purposely close, then hit her from behind as she glanced through the door.

How had she ended up back in her room and in her bed?

As eager as she was to find out the truth, she was aware that a lot of preparations were still to be made for the ball, and that she would need plenty of rest to keep a clear head. Her hands were shaking in anticipation of the day's events. While her stomach churned, her thoughts drifted back to the past. How she had longed to be a part of the dancing. Her coming out ball had proved a disappointment being so soon engaged to Mr Lattimer, thereafter. Now she was to be a hostess of the very first ball at Closings since her husband had taken over as master. How much would be expected of her?

As she reached the wardrobe, she pulled out the ruffled ball gown. She remembered how excited she had been when it arrived from Paris a week ago. She spread the gown out over her figure in front of the full-length mirror, and pictured herself dancing at the ball, her body rocking from side to side, blurring the balayage of salmon and green satin.

Looking across to her husband's room, she wondered if he were awake and feeling as nervous as she was. If he would be pained by the memory of former balls held here before the tragic death of his mother and father. She had begun to feel a little pity for him ever since her conversation with Mrs Radcliffe about the old ballroom, despite his rough ways.

She put away the dress and picked up the book she was part-way through reading as she sauntered back to her bed.

Fluffing up the pillows, she began to read.

Naima found her slumped over her book, asleep, when she entered a few hours later. She threw open the curtains and the bright sunshine that streaked in awoke Scarlett.

"Naima," she said, in a daze and clutching at her neck that ached even more after the awkward position she'd slept in.

"Good morning," Naima said, spinning around.

"Morning, Naima."

"Awake early, I see," Naima said, taking up the book that was lying on top of the duvet.

"I awoke rather early, and I couldn't sleep for thinking about the ball and everything to be done," Scarlett said.

"Nervous, I'll bet? I would be myself, but I know you will be exquisite. You're such an elegant lady, and you will fit in well," Naima said.

"I wish I could have your confidence, Naima, but I appreciate your faith in me. It helps to know you are on my side."

"You will be fine. I'm sure of it." As Naima drew closer to pat her knees, she jumped back and said, "Hey, you look a bit peaky. Hope you're not sickening for something." Naima carefully ran a hand across Scarlett's forehead. "Stone cold."

Scarlett carefully removed her hand. "I'm fine. Don't fuss so much."

Naima's hand flew to her hip. "If, you're sure. I'll be right up with your breakfast."

The day passed slowly in terms of the preparations and Scarlett had a lot of spare time on her hands while Mrs Radcliffe took charge and saw everything ran smoothly.

The housekeeper seemed no different in her behaviour to her mistress and the first storm clouds of doubt were forming in Scarlett's mind if it really was Mrs Radcliffe she followed last night. *If not her, then who?*

But Scarlett knew the housekeeper well enough to know when she was hiding something. She was good at keeping secrets for the master. Scarlett suddenly felt a strong urge to visit the old ballroom again, making her feet itch. She considered that as everybody was busy downstairs she wouldn't be missed if she was to slip away for a while.

Glancing over her shoulder at the room currently used as the ballroom, it struck her then how very different the two rooms were. It was interesting how the fashions of a few decades changed so drastically. The new colours were much brighter and elegant in white and gold with pink panels. The shimmering gold of the chandelier was in the latest style of six lights.

She observed Violet Ellingham, who had returned at dinner last night, talking animatedly at the servants and strutting about the room to instruct them.

No, she would not be missed.

She slipped from the room, and just as she'd made it to the foot of the staircase, a firm voice startled her. "I would like to hear your input as you are the mistress here, not Mrs Ellingham."

It was Mrs Radcliffe.

Scarlett turned around slowly; her hand still planted firmly on the handrail. She stared at the housekeeper in consternation.

Mrs Radcliffe's face had the usual stern appearance, lips taut and hands faithfully by the sides of her black garment.

Scarlett hesitated.

Was this some kind of desperate ploy to stop her snooping once again? Or had it something to do with the strong rivalry between Mrs Radcliffe and Violet?

Sighing, she followed Mrs Radcliffe to the ballroom.

Later it was confirmed Scarlett's input was not needed. She found herself nodding along to Violet's suggestions and even repeating them. She couldn't understand the hold that woman had over her.

Eventually, the hands of the clock reached five-thirty, and it was time to get ready.

After Naima had dressed her, she descended the staircase. Her husband turned his head and their eyes met. There was a look of admiration in his gaze, and he seemed stunned by the way the low cut of the neckline allowed her elongated ringlets to drape across the curvature of her clavicle.

"I knew you would make a fine adornment at Closings, my dear," he whispered in her ear when she reached his side. The warmth in his tone surprised her.

She blushed modestly in reply and his lip curled into an amused smile.

The guests started to flow in now, and amongst them were Mr and Mrs Henson, Lord and Lady Salisbury, the Earl and Duchess of Simms, and Mr and Mrs Kettering.

Catherine came in on the arm of a fair-haired man with a round boyish face and blue eyes in a military uniform. "Scarlett, may I introduce to you my fiancé, Captain Thomas Jepson?"

"I'm so happy to meet you, Captain Jepson," Scarlett said.

"And I you, Mrs Lattimer," he said in a serene tone, taking her hand.

He was followed by Romone Martin.

Scarlett stepped back in surprise. "I never expected to see you here," she said, breaking into a smile.

Mr Lattimer turned his head sharply in his direction. The old threat returned to his mind, and he scowled.

"Miss Henson. I mean, Mrs Lattimer, naturally," Romone said, correcting himself.

"It is so good to see you again," Scarlett said.

"It's a pleasure to see you too. I'm a friend of the captain... But we will talk later," he said, noticing the crowd pressing in on them.

The welcoming over, Mr Lattimer offered Scarlett his arm. The couple led the crowd into the ballroom. The dancing began with a Viennese Waltz. Scarlett had wondered ever since seeing the old ballroom why the portraits of the family were not brought in here. She thought, perhaps they would bring back too many painful memories for her husband.

"Why did she marry him?" Romone said to Catherine, his cheeks glowing as they watched the couple dance from the sidelines.

"It was her choice, though I think her mother wanted it more," Catherine replied.

"She said her mother would marry her off to the first rich man in sight," Romone said.

"I'm afraid Mrs Henson cares for wealth and influence over anything else," Catherine said.

"Why did Scarlett not stand up to her?" Romone asked.

"Oh, she did, but she is so principled, and she wouldn't let obligation pass her by."

"It is a fine quality. She has not been rewarded for it, so it seems."

"She truly has the sweetest heart. Why, when she told me of her engagement, she said she would make the best of the situation. She has done what she set out to do and she's used her influence to benefit the poor. I greatly admire her for it."

"Indeed. You are a good friend to her, Catherine. You should continue to be a friend to her. She needs all the help she can get."

"It is sweet of you to notice," she said, placing a hand on his shoulder.

Once Scarlett had finished dancing, she moved across the room to her friends.

"My dear Scarlett! You have not changed much at all. I'm sure you cannot say the same to me," Romone said.

"I can indeed," Scarlett replied.

"It has been too long. Alas! I should have visited you sooner," Romone said.

"Well, I'm sure you've been busy."

"Yes, for my sins," he said with a laugh, to which Scarlett joined in, causing Mr Lattimer to look her way with distaste.

Scarlett's parents caught her eye, and they came across to speak with them. Mr Henson talked animatedly to Romone.

FROM ACROSS THE ROOM, Violet stared fiercely at the group, making disapproving remarks to her nephew. "What a humiliating spectacle. Scarlett's behaviour does not in the least bit surprise me, but her mother! I thought she would know better than to make such a pointed partiality known to the whole room."

"I believe my wife is besotted with him," her nephew said, with a jealous rage whelming up inside him. Mr Henson's unusual manner seemed to confirm his words.

"You must speak to her about it. Exposing us to such gossip. It is ill-advised, indeed," Violet said.

"I intend to, but for now I must play the fool."

It had been an age since he felt the sting of jealousy in his breast. That's what motivated his thoughts at that moment. He spent the rest of the evening pondering what his next move should be.

CHAPTER TWENTY

Scarlett had danced with Romone many times, enjoying herself so immensely that she paid no heed to what others thought of her.

Once the dancing was done, they sat down to a fine banquet in the dining hall. Scarlett sat by Mr Lattimer at the head of the table. Romone Martin sat on Scarlett's left-hand side, and they talked throughout the meal. Scarlett's eyes were glued to his face whenever he made a remark while her husband kept up a gloomy silence.

The ball ended around midnight and the guests gradually dispersed. Mr and Mrs Henson were the last to leave.

Violet Ellingham was staying the night again, and she would stay on for the rest of the week. She gave her nephew a significant look that Scarlett did not understand before retiring to her room, calling for her lady's maid to join her. Scarlett was about to follow, when Mr Lattimer took her arm, rather too firmly, leading her into the drawing room.

"Sit down. I have something to say to you," he said, his voice booming.

She complied with drooped shoulders.

He walked to the mantel shelf and threw off all the objects resting there. Scarlett winced at the sound of splintering glass as a vase broke into tiny pieces on the hearth. She remained firmly in her seat.

"Have you no shame? No sense of propriety at all? Or are you determined to make a fool of me?" he said, glaring at her through the mirror.

Scarlett could do nothing but stare at him, her emerald eyes wide and shining.

"Are you going to answer me?" he continued.

"I don't know what you are referring to," she said, steadying her voice.

"Can it be possible you're unaware of what your conduct has been this evening?" he said, turning to her with wild eyes.

"My conduct? I'm sure I've done nothing to reproach myself for," she said, feeling herself sincere.

"What of Romone Martin?" he asked.

"Is that what this is about?"

"Are you in love with him?"

"You are jealous," she said.

"I have a right to know as your husband. Are you lovers?"

"Of course not," she said, raising herself up with wounded dignity.

He smiled and shook his head. "No. I forgot you are a principled person entirely, that is why you accepted me. Is it not?"

"You don't understand what you are saying. Your aunt has put you up to this. I know because the two of you have done nothing but scheme against me from the moment we arrived back from Italy."

He paced the floor as she had seen him do in his study.

"I have not seen Romone since our wedding, so it is hardly possible for us to be lovers. He is a dear friend, that is all. I admit there was a time I liked him a lot, but no longer," she said.

A pause followed.

"Then why invite him tonight?" Frank asked, lowering his voice.

She cradled her head. "I didn't know he was coming; besides, I am the mistress of this house, and as such, I will invite whom I please."

"Go to bed," he said, pointing to the entrance.

She rushed from the room as the pent-up tears began to fall, colliding with Mrs Radcliffe on the way out.

"Be careful. You might set your dress on fire," Mrs Radcliffe said, shielding the candlestick.

"Sorry, Mrs Radcliffe."

Scarlett paused midway up the staircase as an impulse struck her. She dashed down again, and after a sharp look around, grabbed a candle from the lamp stand in the hallway. She ran to the secret passageway and pushed on the picture, ducking inside when it swung open. The passage was much easier to manage now she had some lighting, so she soon reached the door to the old ballroom.

Once inside, she glided to the portraits hanging on the wall, throwing some light upon them. The first picture she came to was that of an elderly gentleman with a long, grey beard who bore no resemblance to Frank. The next few pictures were likewise unrecognisable until the candlelight fell on a family portrait with one of the ladies strongly resembling Violet Ellingham. A young boy of about five-years-old with fair hair and blue eyes sat on her knee. She recalled Violet telling Lady Salisbury that was the age of Frank when his parents were killed, yet the boy in the portrait did not resemble her husband in any way.

Frank was dark, not fair!

And while it was true that people changed as they aged, they did not generally change that much. Who was this boy? Where was Frank?

She shone the candle further along the wall, searching the faces, but she found none resembling her husband.

She started as she suddenly became aware of a firm hand on her shoulder, and she spun around, causing the candle to fall from its holder, and extinguish on the floor.

CHAPTER TWENTY-ONE

"Madam?" echoed the sharp, clear voice of Mrs Radcliffe out of the blackness.

"Mrs Radcliffe I. . . I lost my way," Scarlett stammered.

A long pause ensued, during which time, Scarlett waited with bated breath.

"You wanted to see it, did you not?" Mrs Radcliffe said at last. Her voice had become deep and mournful in the empty space between them.

Scarlett gaped. "I did, yes."

She was beginning to doubt if it really had been the housekeeper she followed last night, for tonight, she seemed to have lost some of her reluctance to show her the west wing. In fact, she seemed almost eager now to share it with her. Scarlett shivered inwardly at the possibility that someone else wanted to prevent her from seeing the room.

Fear tangled in her breast, making her eyes wide at the idea that her husband had tried to prevent her. There was thus no hope for their marriage if this was the case. The hope that had once calmed her mind of a reconciliation between them, died with the thought.

"I feel there is some history here that is deliberately kept from me," Scarlett said, truthfully.

"You wish to hear more about the Lattimer family?" Mrs Radcliffe asked.

"I do."

"Wait here while I get another candle," Mrs Radcliffe said, disappearing down the passageway. She reappeared moments later carrying a candle. "I was lucky to have kept it lit until nightfall. I usually extinguish them much earlier, but with the ball finishing at midnight, I was delayed this evening."

"I see," Scarlett said.

"This portrait is of the Earl of Somersby, who was not connected to the Lattimer family," Mrs Radcliffe said, pointing to the first picture they came to. "The first member of the Lattimer family to live here was the master's great-grandfather, and he can be seen in this portrait here," Mrs Radcliffe continued, shining her candle on a portrait higher than the rest. "Mrs Ellingham can be seen to the right here in her much younger days."

The candle lit upon a lady of about five and twenty dressed in an elegant robe. Only the eyes gave away the identity of the wearer very clearly.

"Oh, she was a very handsome young lady," Scarlett exclaimed.

"Indeed, she was, madam. Here is the portrait of Mr and Mrs George Lattimer. Their son, Frank, sits here on his mother's lap," she said, pointing to the fair-haired boy.

"Frank has changed quite a lot, hasn't he? This boy is fair."

Mrs Radcliffe's lips tightened. "He has."

"What happened to his parents?"

"They were killed in the infamous fire of eighteen hundred and two."

"The fire, of course. How did it happen?"

"I'm not entirely sure. It started in this part of the castle, which was more frequently used in those days. It was most likely a candle blowing over. I heard screams coming from the room at the end of the corridor where the family used to sit in the evening to watch the lake. There was once a fine balcony there, but the room has never recovered after the fire, and it has stayed the same ever since," Mrs Radcliffe said.

"Was Frank injured in the fire?"

"No, but it has scarred him inwardly for life. That is why he cannot bear to be anywhere near this part of the castle."

Scarlett glanced at the paintings on the wall. "Why are there no portraits of my husband anywhere in the castle?"

"He hasn't had one painted. It is getting late, we had better return now," the housekeeper said, hurriedly showing her out.

A WEEK AFTER THE BALL, Violet joined her nephew for breakfast before making her departure. She was in the middle of outlining her plan to him when Scarlett came downstairs after having breakfast in her room.

"I should put on a show of friendliness towards her. That should do it," Violet whispered hurriedly, finishing her orange juice.

"Ah, Scarlett. There you are," Violet said, coming into the entranceway.

Scarlett was taken aback by her cheery tone of voice, and she paused at the foot of the stairs a few moments before following Violet outside.

"What a great success last night was. I was just telling Frank I needn't have worried about a thing," Violet continued when Mr Lattimer had retreated to his study.

Scarlett had not expected this. What could be the reason for her sudden turn for kindness?

She was even more startled when Violet pulled her into an embrace, and she felt herself freeze as the aunt's long fingers nestled at the nape of her neck, patting the exact spot where she was hit.

It was Violet who hit her, not Mrs Radcliffe.

She must have been desperate to hide the clues that were buried with the fire in the old room, once so beloved that she was trying to sweet-talk her.

Scarlett instantly pulled away. She breathed a sigh of relief as the carriage conveyed the aunt away from them.

LONDON, 1832

In front of the oval mirror, decorated in gold leaf carvings, Violet lifted a shaking hand to her face. She saw the fire in her eyes, and her late husband's face burning bright.

Her fingers clutched the folded cotton neckline of the wide dress she wore. Her marriage had been a swift union. She'd met Mr Ellingham at the Closings annual ball. Across the dance floor, he'd offered her an escape from the sorrows that clouded her brow as a young girl. They were tolerably content, but she knew she'd have been happier with her first love, and even though it was Jane Salisbury who'd spoiled her chance of happiness when she interrupted their elopement, she had to admit she and Lord Salisbury made a handsome couple.

Violet held a grudge against Lady Salisbury for a long while. Her family had dwindled, but at least Frank offered her some consolation, even if the wife he'd chosen didn't sit comfortably with her. She was far too impulsive for her liking, and everything Violet had to conceal, Scarlett was gradually bringing to the surface. She clutched at the dressing table. No one must ever find out. She would give anything to make sure of that.

CHAPTER TWENTY-TWO

The castle had settled down after the whirlwind of Violet's visit. Scarlett found herself pondering the change to her husband's mood whenever it was that his aunt left them.

"The servants are talking of Mrs Ellingham's visit between them," Naima said to her as she dressed her hair for the afternoon.

Scarlett spun around.

"Careful," Naima said as a placement pin pulled out a lock of her hair with the action.

Scarlett was spun back to face the mirror by her shoulders.

Naima smoothed some hair into place, and sliding the pin from between her teeth, she gripped it tightly to Scarlett's scalp. "Is there something you're not telling me about Mrs Ellingham?"

"I'm not sure," Scarlett said with a sigh. "There's something about her presence that sends a chill down my spine."

"That's how the servants put it, especially Mrs Radcliffe," she said and then plunged into her account of what took place in the servants' quarters between Redwood and her during her stay.

"Did Mrs Radcliffe say what these papers were?" Scarlett asked, turning pale.

That's what she was looking for in her sitting room that day.

Naima shook her head. "Violet had asked specifically for them. When Mrs Ellingham confirmed it later, Mrs Radcliffe couldn't argue, but she put up a heck of a fight, I can tell you. I think she's met her match at long last."

"That sounds like Mrs Radcliffe."

"Yes, but she's too discreet. Wouldn't you agree?" Naima asked.

"At least we have that in common. She wants to protect the Lattimer's reputation, as do I," Scarlett said.

"Well, I suppose it's not a bad thing."

"No, indeed.

"But that's the only way the two of you compare. You could never grow to be so stiff and cold," Naima said.

Scarlett grimaced thinking of her earlier dream about her heart turning to stone. "Let us hope not."

LATER THAT DAY, SCARLETT was making her usual rounds visiting with the poor when she came across the same old man who was spying on her in Stanton Moore. She met him in the lane walking his dog. The fresh air had made his face ruddy, and now she saw him more closely, one of his eyes appeared to be missing, which would explain why he fixed her with a slanting gaze.

"Come you," he said to the bulldog as it sniffed at Scarlett's ankles. He pointed a grubby finger firmly on the ground. "Heel!"

The dog ignored his command and ran along the lane.

"Good morning, sir," she called politely as he started to walk away.

"You don't want to go talking to the likes of me, ma'am," he said, turning slightly, his voice gravelly.

"What is your name?" she asked.

"William Morrison. You're from the castle, aren't you?" he said, fixing one narrowed eye on her.

"That's right, Mr Morrison. I am Mrs Lattimer," she said, holding out her hand to him, but he waved it away.

"Strange business, that. I pity you," he said, shaking his head, his bristled hair bobbing from side to side.

"What is that Mr Morrison? What is strange?" she asked.

"It was a strange business, all right," he muttered a second time.

"What was?" she asked in a quavering voice.

He walked away from her. Scarlett followed at his heels, pulling her tartan cape tighter around her as a gust of wind blew down the lane.

"Mr Morrison, if there is some knowledge you possess about Closings, please tell me," she said.

"It isn't my place. I'll be getting along," he said, disappearing.

She struggled to catch up with him, battling against the wind. When she turned the corner, he was gone.

She turned back, deep disappointment gnawing away inside her.

Upon inquiring about Mr Morrison at the Farley cottage where she next visited, she learnt that he had once served as Head Gardener at the castle. Scarlett's eyes sparkled with interest as Mrs Farley told her about him while she mangled the laundry in the kitchen sink. "It was many moons ago, and he always had copious stories to tell, whether any of them were true is yet to be seen," Mrs Farley said.

"Do you think he could tell me more about the fire?" Scarlett asked, watching the children play at her feet.

"It's possible. It was him who told me those other stories, but, like I said, I'm not sure if he can be relied upon," Mrs Farley said, tapping her temple. "Not quite right in the head. Never was."

"A MR MARTIN IS WAITING for you in your sitting room," Larsson informed her, back at the castle.

"Thank you, Larsson," she said with a bright smile, relieved that she would enjoy some cheerful and honest company for a change.

"Romone! How good it is to see you," she said, bursting into the sitting room.

He rose to greet her. "I'm glad to see you alone, Scarlett. I feel we have much to catch up on." He twisted his hat. "Your husband is out, I believe?" he asked.

"Yes, but there is no need to worry about Frank. Shall I order us some tea?" she said, her finger poised to ring the bell.

He thanked her, inclining his head to tell her he would refuse her offer. "I think a turn in the grounds would suit me better on such a fine day as this," he said, glancing at the long stretch of wilderness.

"Shall we?" She led the way to the patio. Naima supplied her with a shawl, and she was escorted on the gravel path, eventually reaching the lake. A row of cedar trees sheltered their path from the sun.

"How are you, Scarlett? Honestly?" Romone asked with a grave face.

"As well as can be expected. Better than the poor I visited this morning. I cannot complain," she said, cheerfully.

"I suppose not, yet you deserved more, I must add."

"More than this?" She indicated the beautiful grounds all around them.

"I don't mean in terms of your situation, but that you deserved more from a husband."

"Frank is a troubled soul, but he is not as some people would have you believe. His threats are far worse than anything he might do," she said, tying the ribbon on her wide-brimmed bonnet

"Nevertheless, you could have aimed higher in terms of love and a little more concern for your welfare," Romone said.

"That may be true. It is done now, however. There's no going back. I believe marriage to be a binding matter. I cannot go back on my word."

"That is admirable, but I fear for your future with that man."

"That man owns this very path we are walking on, so I would be careful what you say about him," she said.

"Indeed, I forget," he said in jest.

"I will be well. Do not fret for me."

"I will try not to."

"Have you heard from Catherine at all? Does she bring any news of the wedding?" Scarlett asked.

"They have set the date for early next summer. It won't be long to wait," Romone said.

"I'm so happy for her. I will eagerly await the invitation in the post."

"Indeed. She has met a fine match in Captain Jepson," he said.

"I believe she has. He has such fine manners, does he not?" she said, smiling.

"He does. I have never known a finer man, and it is a pleasure to be his friend."

"That is a fine testimony coming from you."

"WHO IS HE?" SARAH SAID, peering through the drawing room window at Scarlett and Romone as they sauntered to the castle together.

"Don't ask me. Some friend. Martin, I think his name is," James said.

Sarah clicked her fingers. "That's it. He was at the ball, wasn't he?"

"They're looking mighty cosy, I must say," James said with a quick glance over his shoulder.

"Eh. They did at the ball too. She made such a show of herself, she did. I heard the master telling her off in the drawing room afterward. Then he called me in to clean up the mess, he did," Sarah said.

James stroked his chin. "Did he now?"

"Right mad, he was."

"We had better get along, Sarah, before we get caught," he hissed as Scarlett approached.

Outside, as Scarlett and Romone reached the front of the castle, Mr Lattimer pulled up in his carriage. His brow darkened, a look that told Scarlett his business in town hadn't gone to plan.

CHAPTER TWENTY-THREE

"Oh, dear," Martin muttered.

"I'll deal with him," Scarlett whispered as her husband alighted.

Frank froze when he caught sight of them and gave them a suspicious, mocking glance.

"Frank, you remember Mr Martin?" Scarlett said when they caught him up.

"Of course. How could I forget?" Frank replied, his lip curled.

"Mr Lattimer," Romone said, holding out his hand.

Frank sneered before turning his back on them. He strode inside the castle.

"That was easy," Romone muttered.

"I must apologise for my husband's behaviour," Scarlett said.

"No, don't. Never apologise to me, Scarlett. I'm the one who should make amends to you. I should have married you myself," Romone said.

"You mustn't say such things. I am a man's wife. It cannot be undone."

"Only someone who is as sweet and as lovely as you would say so."

"Don't speak like this. There can never be anything between us. We were not meant to be together, you and I," she said, resting a hand on his arm.

"How can we know that now?" Romone asked, he gripped the silver handle of his walking stick.

"I just know it. I'm equally as sure that one day you will meet someone you were meant to be with," Scarlett said.

"I'm not so confident."

"Please, believe me," Scarlett said, tears forming on her eyelashes.

"If it will make you happy," he said, prodding the ground with the stick.

"It will."

"I must go now. Goodbye and good luck," he said, kissing the hand she held out to him.

His horse was brought around from the stables, and with the help of the stable boy, he mounted with a grim look. As he galloped away, he called something over his shoulder that sounded very much like, "I'll return soon. Don't you fret."

Immediately upon entering the castle, Scarlett sought out her husband. She was informed that he had gone to change for lunch, so she waited until they were dining to broach the subject of his conduct with poor Romone.

"You were very rude, darling. I don't think he has done anything to deserve such treatment," she began tactfully, taking a sip of wine.

"I don't think it is your place to comment on my manners, darling. I will treat people how I see fit," he replied, taking steaming potatoes from the server and positioning them on his plate.

"To all appearances it would seem strange that you should do so," she said.

Frank wiped at the corners of his mouth with a napkin. He rested his hands beside his plate. "Look, I do not want the man here. That is all."

"But he was my guest. I believe guests should be treated cordially. Is that not one of the first rules of society that you think it necessary to follow?" she asked.

"Society would also see your conduct as negligent, my dear."

"How could it?"

Lattimer's eyes sought out her face. "Because it would appear he is your lover. Whether it is true or not, that is how they will see it. I don't want you to incite gossip."

Scarlett's cheeks grew hot. "You know it is not true. I told you that myself."

Lattimer frowned and looked away. "Nevertheless, I must ask you not to receive him here again."

"I don't think that will be necessary, as he will not come here again after your treatment of him, anyway."

Lattimer ignored her comment, leaning back in his chair. When he spoke again, his voice became more earnest. There was even a tinge of concern in it. He leaned forward, taking her hand. "I'm concerned for your honour. I know I speak roughly sometimes, but you must be sensible."

She gripped his hand. "I hope you always see me as rational."

"I don't doubt it, but we all need guidance. I speak from my heart. I want the best for you," he said.

Frank was summoned by Larsson, who informed him that Mr Serengeti had arrived and was waiting in his study.

Scarlett unwillingly let go of his hand. A need to be near him was new to her.

He grinned before disappearing from the room.

She left the table and crossed paths with the butler on her way out. "Larsson, I'm going for a walk if anybody asks for me."

He bowed.

She changed into a pair of cubic walking shoes, then followed Mrs Farley's directions to William Morrison's cottage.

When she reached her destination, the grinding stone attached to the cottage told her it had once been a working mill. The surrounding canal moat made her wonder how she would reach the other side.

Going further forward, she came to a swaying bridge. Biting her lip, she placed her foot on the first plank of wood over the cloudy water. The sound of splitting wood made her draw back before it caved in altogether.

What to do.

She called Mr Morrison's name across the water.

Eventually, his head popped out of the upstairs window.

As she explained her position, he grunted for her to be on her way, beginning to close the window.

"Wait! Is there another way?" she asked.

He opened the window wider. "There's a footpath through those trees." He pointed to the thick foliage beside her, slamming the window.

Peering through the bare trees, she found out Mr Morrison was telling the truth. Carefully manoeuvring the branches, stopping occasionally to untangle her cape before pressing on. When she made it to the other side, she found herself on a winding lane that turned into a path to Mr Morrison's garden. She paused to pull loose twigs off her dress before proceeding to his front door.

When she was permitted to enter, after some argument on the part of Mr Morrison, she found the cottage to be dusty, but she ignored this and chose to stay to find out what he knew.

"What can I do for you, Mrs Lattimer?" he asked, retrieving newspapers from a chair and waving her to it.

She refused to sit when she noticed how dusty the chairs were.

The dog gave a high-pitched howl from the adjoining room. Mr Morrison asked fiercely for it to be quiet.

"I heard you were Head Gardener at Closings around the time of the fire, Mr Morrison?" she asked, standing in his kitchen that was piled high with used pottery.

"I was that. What of it?" He grabbed a cup, the only one left in the cupboard, and offered to make her some tea.

She shook her head. "I'm interested in the history of the castle. I wonder if you would consider telling me your story?"

"I'm not going to fall for that nonsense. I have been fooled by women before now," he said.

"I am not trying to fool you, Mr Morrison."

He rubbed his head. "Aren't you, though? Then why don't you ask your husband the story? Answer me that."

"Mr Morrison. I think you know the answer."

"You think you can learn more from me, don't you?" He stared at her.

"Of course. A gardener would get acquainted with the goings-on in such an estate," she said.

"I'm not going to give up any secrets, mind. I have my loyalty, I do."

"Then you must be loyal to me. I am part of the family now." She moved her head closer to him and gazed into his eyes.

The expression in his own eyes softened. "All right. I will tell you what I can."

"Please do, Mr Morrison," she said.

"I must begin from when I first came. It was fifty years ago when I got the post. I was your age. I was excited, like, about starting out in such a fine castle," he said, stopping as he gazed out of the window.

Scarlett followed his gaze.

When he looked her way, nostalgia had crept into his eyes. "Mrs Radcliffe wasn't there when I began. It was a Mrs Peters in Mr Lattimer's grandfather's time. He was called Frank as well, and his lady wife, Annabelle. I was happy there. Treated me well, they did. I got on with my work mostly, you know?" I liked to watch genteel folk coming and going. The standards dropped in Mrs Radcliffe's time. She arrived forty years ago when old Mr Lattimer was getting on a bit, then he died and his son, George, took over. He was a stroppy lad. It was never the same after that. I suppose that's where the current master gets his manners from. Begging your pardon, I'm sure," he said.

She bowed her head in forgiveness.

"Named for his grandfather, Frank was. Then the tragedy happened thirty years ago. I disliked the man, but it was a shame, nonetheless. His wife was Mrs Ellingham's sister. Miss Isabella Danforth was her maiden name. A genteel lady, always ailing, but there was no harm in her." Mr Morrison paused in his narration, folding his arms and deliberating if he should continue his story or not.

"When did you leave Closings, Mr Morrison?" Scarlett asked.

"After the fire when Mrs Ellingham took Frank away. I could not go on working there. Not after that. Mrs Radcliffe wanted me to carry on like, keep the place ticking over a bit. A few of them carried on a while until they closed it up. Mrs Radcliffe went away to London to work for a big house up there until Frank took it on again," he said.

"Is there something else I should be aware of, Mr Morrison? For I feel there is something I'm missing?" she asked.

William Morrison shuffled uneasily on his feet and refused to meet her gaze.

"There are still some gaps somewhere in the history of Closings," she said.

He shook his head. "I don't know much. This is all I can tell you."

"Why was the castle closed? Surely Frank could have stayed on with his aunt? The house is practically run by Mrs Radcliffe," she said.

"I cannot tell. You must leave the past alone. If I have learnt anything in life, it is that. You must be getting along now, ma'am," he said.

"But I have one last question for you, Mr Morrison. Did you notice anything unusual before you left Closings?" She looked longingly into his eyes.

He blinked. After some hesitation, he spoke. "I swear to you that three bodies were pulled out of the fire."

CHAPTER TWENTY-FOUR

Three bodies?

What can this mean?

As she strode up to the castle, Scarlett mulled over the gardener's ramblings in her mind. Mr Morrison said he had tried to save the family from the balcony, but it had been too late. He was certain he had seen three bodies being carried out. Mrs Ellingham had said she took Frank to his room to recover immediately after the fire where the doctor would see him. She did not know the gardener had seen the bodies.

The suspicion his testimony conjured up in her mind was too fearful to even contemplate. A scandal of this magnitude would ruin her for sure. What had she got herself mixed up in? What would her mama say? She surely wouldn't have sought the match so fervently if she'd known of this. She had to bear the burden alone and the decision about her next move rested entirely on her shoulders.

Arriving at the castle, Scarlett went to her room where she found Naima waiting for her.

"Where have you been? The master was looking for you," Naima asked, almost tearing out her own hair.

"I cannot tell you," Scarlett replied, untying her cape, which then fell straight into Naima's outstretched hands.

"How intriguing," Naima said as she hung the cloak in the closet.

Scarlett paced the floor, a hand on the pointed bodice of her gown. "Naima, can I ask a favour of you?"

"Anything you like."

"Could you keep an eye out for Frank, or his valet while I search his room?"

Naima's eyes widened. "Search his room? Why would you ever do that?"

"I need to find something," Scarlett said.

"What do you need to find?"

"I'm not sure, but I must find something."

"If you insist on it. Are you quite well?" Naima asked, running a hand across Scarlett's forehead.

"Fine, Naima. Will you keep a lookout for me?" Scarlett asked.

"How shall I alert you if someone is coming?"

"Knock quietly on the door."

"Right you are, mistress. I will get to my post."

Scarlett used the adjoining door, tiptoeing to Frank's wardrobe. She searched through the pockets of his clothes. Finding nothing of interest, she tried the drawers. Still, she found nothing.

During a second attempt, her hand brushed against a hidden compartment.

She felt her pulse quicken. Her breaths came thick and fast.

Just as she was about to pull the compartment open, she heard a light tapping. She started, hearing her husband's heavy footsteps sounding on the stairs.

Hastily closing the drawer, she dashed back to her room. She had a chance to close the door before she heard her husband enter.

Naima rushed in, breathless and leaned against the closed door. "Well, that was close. Did you find anything?"

"Almost. I must ask you again, I'm afraid."

"Oh, you will give me a heart attack. Let's get you into your dress for dinner."

TO ADD WEIGHT TO THE secret, a storm brewed outside as they took their places at the table. The rain thudded on the roof.

Dinner was over almost before it had begun as a booming echo resounded on the castle door as soon as the starters came out of the kitchen.

It would not let up.

Larsson barged into the dining room, breathless. As he spluttered out an explanation, the farmer from Parsons Farm pushed past him and told them all in a calm, concise tone what had happened. Only his ruddy complexion gave away any signs of the turmoil within.

"It's my hay barn, Mr Lattimer, sir. The storm has blown the thatched roof right off, and it's like to be blown asunder by the wind. I need help securing it again or else my feed for a year is all gone, and my livestock will suffer. It is a two-man job, and my assistant is indisposed. There are no hired hands that can come out to us tonight. Otherwise, I wouldn't have troubled you. I must beg the master for his help, or my livelihood is down the drain," the farmer said.

Frank removed the napkin from his lapel. "Who gave you permission to enter?"

"I apologise, but my situation is desperate," Farmer Jasper said.

Scarlett placed a hand on her husband's arm, pleading with her eyes. "Please," she mouthed. "Can't you see he is helpless?"

Frank hesitated, his expression gradually softening. "Oh, dash it. Take us to them."

Scarlett's fist pumped the air. They hastily left the table together.

Outside, the storm was well underway, the wind battering their clothes and hair as they dashed across fields to get to Parsons Farm, struggling to keep up with Farmer Jasper's quickened pace. The drops of water glimmered on the damp grass, a mossy smell becoming more prevalent with each step.

When they reached the farm, seeing the strands of hay scattered across the ground, Frank stripped off his dinner jacket, rolling up his shirt sleeves. "We can save them! Fetch us some string to tie around them," he said to Scarlett as he climbed the ladder.

She nodded and ran towards a wooden shed, flinging the door open while clinging on to the latch to stop it blowing away.

Pinning the door shut, she fell against the entrance, listening to a ringing in her ears as the silence hit her with only a faint whistling sound still present, a reminder that there was still a storm outside.

Frantically searching the shed, she found the blue thread hanging on a rusty nail on the wall, as well as a hammer and some nails to secure the bales in place. Next, she found some fabric to act as a temporary cover until Jasper could get the roof fixed.

Running back to the hay barn, she got soaked to the skin as the rain started to come down thick and fast. Slipping in the soft mud that had become like a thick clay, she unravelled the string. Almost losing her footing, she fought to keep her balance, thrashing her hands about in the air.

Frank dived off the ladder and latched onto her waist, steadying her and just managing to avoid falling headfirst into the mud himself. "I've got you," he said.

"I'll survive," she assured him, her hair sticking to her skin.

While Scarlett held on tight, Frank and Jasper used the string to carefully weave it around the delicate strands in a bundle. They tied them into a tight knot, and as a nurse assisting a doctor, Scarlett handed them nails so they could hammer them down.

As he gathered the string, Scarlett looked at Frank. She realised this was the first time they'd worked together on anything. It got her blood pumping, and it could almost have been his farm and her the farmer's wife.

The bundles all secured and safe, they nailed the fabric covering to the top of the barn. They were hurriedly thanked by the farmer as they ran for shelter under a nearby canopy, the water droplets splashing around their feet. They clung to each other, laughing as they tried to avoid the splashes and getting wetter than they already were. Scarlett screeched as a gust of wind blew the heavy downpour beneath the canopy.

As their heads drew closer, Scarlett reached up to his face, tenderly brushing a patch of stray dirt from his cheek. Her hand lingered as she stared up at him, her blushed lips quivering. For a moment Frank thought she was going to kiss him, until a bleating lamb stirred her compassion in another direction. As the rain had almost stopped, she reunited the lost lamb with its mother. Dragging Frank gently by the hand, they made their escape to the castle. With one last lingering look between them, they parted on the top step of the staircase.

As Scarlett made it to her room, a giddiness overtook her and her step felt lighter as if she were walking on air, her stomach churning. For the first time in her life, she felt what it was to be in love. She felt a sudden desire to be near Frank. A longing to pour out her heart to him for the first time since they met.

IN HIS ROOM, FRANK untied his soaking lapel and threw his wet shirt on the ground. Droplets splayed his skin. Going to the wash tub he found a neatly folded towel and dried himself.

Scarlett's upturned face haunted his mind. Even she, who had once married him out of pure convenience and principle couldn't have missed the bond that had formed between them tonight. Why did they have to be interrupted? She'd wanted him to kiss her. How he wished he'd swept her up into his arms before she could escape.

His palms were clammy, his eyes darting about.

The secret he bore was too important to disclose, even to the woman he loved.

Could he risk everything by getting too close to her?

THE NEXT DAY, SCARLETT waited for her husband to go out before slipping into his room, keeping Naima at her post as a precaution.

She immediately walked over to the drawer with the hidden compartment, more curious than ever after a restless night of wondering. With confidence she pulled it open, and it swung out smoothly. A tawny leather folder was revealed to her.

Her hands trembled as she opened the sleeve. She hesitated before looking inside.

Since the awakening of love for Frank, she hoped with all her strength to be proved wrong in her suspicions, for Mr Morrison's story to be a wicked lie told to discredit the family, but since she respected the gardener a lot, she found it hard to believe.

Steadying her breath, she slid her hand inside the folder.

She found a small portrait of a young boy amongst the papers. The dark eyes staring back at her were familiar. On the back, a single name, Tom.

She studied the boy's features closely.

Who is Tom?

She also found a birth certificate inside, along with the portrait, and it had the name Thomas Danforth written upon it. The parents were Ray Banks and Violet Danforth. She recalled that Danforth was Violet Ellingham's maiden name.

So, it would seem Tom is her illegitimate child. But where is Tom now and how come she had never heard him mentioned?

She studied the features of the dark boy in the portrait again, even though, deep down, she knew the answer. As she thought, the question was answered in his wild eyes looking back at her.

She was in no doubt.

She felt the sting of anger when she considered the reasons that had led her to marry in the first place. Likewise, she knew her influence in the town was obsolete if she was not who she thought she was. Why, she was nothing but the wife of a pauper who lived at Closings under false pretenses.

Why had they lied to her and her family about his identity? How could they resort to such deception for their own ends?

The other document in the folder appeared to be the will of Mr George Lattimer. The next one in line to inherit Closings and his large fortune after Frank Lattimer, was to be a John Danforth, on the condition that Mrs Lattimer had no more children.

Keeping the contents out, she pushed the folder back into the compartment of the drawer and pushed it shut.

She went to assess the situation in the castle. Naima informed her that Mr Lattimer had not yet returned and that Mrs Radcliffe was in her sitting room. She was usually there for a good half an hour.

Scarlett made her way to the west wing and into the old ballroom to look at the portraits again.

MRS PHILIPS CARRIED a basket of provisions into the kitchen she bought from the village that morning. As she selected the items for the lunch she was about to prepare, she was startled by a man with a rough beard, wearing wellies six inches deep in mud. She dived back a few paces, reaching for a long-handled brush to show him off the property.

It was Farmer Jasper who hastened to introduce himself, taking off his cap and staring sheepishly with speckled blue eyes.

"I don't care who you are, you're not traipsing mud through here," she said, guarding the entrance.

He rubbed his thick neck, saying, "I was hoping to have a word with your mistress."

"Not dressed like that you're not."

"Can you send for her, please? It won't take long."

"I suppose that can be arranged with Larsson, but it is most irregular," Mrs Philips said, waggling out of sight. She came back with Larsson marching behind her.

"What is this?" Larsson asked.

The butler's eyes bulged out of his head when the farmer explained what he wanted. "It is most improper to ask the mistress of this castle to enter the servants' kitchen. I will not allow it."

"Don't worry, Larsson. Let me deal with this," Scarlett's voice startled him from the entrance.

Larsson pressed a hand to his forehead and bowed stiffly. He marched the way he had come.

Mrs Philips retreated to the larder.

"I was on my way to see the housekeeper when I heard your voice," Scarlett said.

Jasper inclined his head in a stiff bow.

"How is your harvest? I hope we secured them well enough," Scarlett asked.

Jasper turned his cap around in his hands. "They're saved, ma'am. I wanted to thank you personally for the service you rendered Mrs Jasper and I, without which, we would never have saved the wheat. I can't tell you how grateful we both are."

"Who else should help our tenants?" she asked.

"You saved my farm. I thank you for persuading Mr Lattimer to help us."

"He would have helped you whatever I said, you can be sure. He does have it in him. However much he tries to portray to you otherwise," she said.

"I hope you're right, for all our sakes. We're thrilled to have you here," he said.

"I'm glad I can be of service after your loyalty to this household," she said.

"Then, let's say no more." He replaced his cap and vanished around the corner.

CHAPTER TWENTY-FIVE

The knowledge she had come to possess, coupled with Mr Morrison's testimony, and the suspicion it all conjured up in her mind, proved too much for Scarlett to bear. She pondered what her next move should be.

By the time she was dressed that morning, she had already decided that her only option was one she disliked the idea of with all her heart. But it had to be done, and she must speak with Mr Serengeti sooner than later.

She journeyed to his office in London upon inquiring about the whereabouts in town.

Struggling to see where she was going through the smoky air, she covered her nose with a handkerchief to avoid breathing in the sulphuric odour carried from the river. Scarlett longed to be back in the beloved country air whenever she visited the city.

The secretary looked surprised but delighted to see her, extending his hands to her as she entered, yet keeping a safe distance away from her.

"I would appreciate it if my husband didn't hear about this visit. I would like to be the one to tell him," she said, settling on a chair.

"Naturally, Signora Lattimer. I am your most obedient servant." He had also settled in a chair, and he held out his hands, his short stature almost getting lost behind the large desk.

"Why has your attitude changed towards me? If I may ask such a question?" she asked.

"I want to help you. Do the best I can, of course," he said.

"Why is that?"

"Because your husband asked me to."

She eyed him doubtfully. "He did?"

"Naturally. He told me not to come near you, and that I was to protect you if it ever became necessary." He arched his fingers as if they were a stack of playing cards, resting them on the bridge of his nose in his usual professional style.

"Why would it be necessary for you to protect me?" she asked.

He shrugged his shoulders. "I can't say why, Signora. But you must know this, your husband loves you with all his heart, with everything he is. You have no need for alarm there." His voice became suddenly animated, heartfelt.

"How do you know this?" she asked distrustfully.

"I've been acquainted with him all his life, Signora, and I asked him outright. He told me he loves you more than his life, and he wants to protect you from the truth. Why should I lie to you?" he asked.

Scarlett felt herself warming to her husband on hearing this speech. Mr Serengeti would have no need to lie to her about this. "I think you need to explain the truth to me, Mr Serengeti. I need to hear your story."

"How much do you know?" he asked.

Scarlett told him of her conversation with William Morrison and of seeing the portrait of Frank Lattimer in the old ballroom, but she left out the further evidence she'd found in the hidden compartment.

"So, you don't know much?" he asked.

"I know enough to have worked out the truth," she said, clasping her hands in her lap.

"I cannot tell you, Signora. I have my loyalty to your husband to consider, and he does not want you to learn the truth. You must ask your husband."

"I must ask you one question," she said.

"And what is that?"

"What did you mean when you said you have known him all his life? You originate in Italy, do you not, sir?" she asked.

He shuffled papers on his desk. "You're correct, Signora. I met your husband while he was a boy in Italy. His great-grandfather originated there many years ago before his grandfather purchased Closings. We became good friends and it stuck until now. We lost touch until I came here as his secretary. The rest is history. This is all the information I can give you." He stood up to usher her out of the room.

"But what of the document you tried to force me to sign?" she asked, getting to her feet.

"You must ask your husband for more, Signora. It can only rightly come from him now."

As she walked out onto the busy London Street, she grappled with mixed feelings of relief that she had her husband's affection, but at the same time a sense of dread ran through her of what she was about to find out about the man she was falling in love with.

She edged further along the street, forgetting the carriage and Travers waiting for her.

"Scarlett!" she heard a sharp voice from behind her say.

She turned around to find Violet Ellingham eyeing her warily from a distance.

"Violet!" Scarlett's steps lessened the gap.

"You have seen Serengeti?" Violet raised her brows.

"No!" On seeing Violet's twisted mouth, she continued, "I mean, yes, I have."

"Hm. What business do you have with him?" Violet asked.

"Please don't tell Frank I was here," Scarlett said, hesitant to pronounce his name.

"Why should I not? You should be aware that I have never liked you, because you are weak, and you need the help of strangers. I have always been strong and so has my nephew. You don't belong at Closings. Why should I do anything for you?" Violet said.

Scarlett dropped her hands, resignedly. "You are right, Mrs Ellingham. I understand you have never liked me. I know what you did when I followed you that night, before the ball. Your secret was so desperate."

Violet proudly drew herself up, giving her the same sharp look Scarlett had seen on their first meeting on Lady Salisbury's grounds.

Mustering up courage, Scarlett continued, "I do not belong in a place where such secrets are harboured, yet it is where life has led me, and so I must stick to it. You do not know me at all if you believe that I am not strong."

A huff came from Violet and her fingers sought the handle of the door to the office Scarlett had lately quitted.

"You have, however, confirmed something for me just now," Scarlett said.

Violet pivoted. Fear flickered in her vision. Her composure soon returned as she replied, "You can know nothing. Serengeti is loyal."

Scarlett bravely lifted her head. "Oh, he is very loyal, yet I have eyes and ears and I can work things out for myself."

"Is that right?" Violet said, her voice a low hiss.

"You may have been wrong before, but I think we can work together for Frank," Scarlett said.

At the mention of Frank's name, Violet breathed deeply, and pointed a finger in Scarlett's face. "I will not let you ruin him. You're nothing but a silly, insignificant girl."

"And the mistress of Closings. Something you will never be," Scarlett said.

"Excuse me. I must speak with Serengeti," Violet replied, but her voice had become a hoarse whisper.

CHAPTER TWENTY-SIX

Larsson frowned on Scarlett's return, informing her that she had missed lunch. She hastened to apologise and tried to disappear before her husband came looking for her.

"Scarlett. Where have you been?" Frank said, appearing in the hallway as she started to mount the stairs.

"Frank," she said, facing him. Her cheeks burned.

"You missed lunch."

"I wasn't hungry, and I had an errand to run," she spoke softly.

"An errand?" He wrinkled his brow.

"Yes, for the poor," she said hurriedly.

He looked unconvinced. "Well, I think I will let it pass this once."

"I must change."

"You should. Your dress looks awfully dusty." He glanced at the dust-rimmed hem of her dress.

"It is," she said, glancing at her feet. She turned her back on him and dashed up the stairs.

He stared after her with a frown until she disappeared.

Later, Scarlett changed into a satin, heavily pleated evening dress. The ivory lace along the neckline set off her complexion to her best advantage. She joined her husband for dinner.

"You are early this evening, darling," he said.

"It seems I am." She avoided his gaze, keeping her eyes fixed on the charcoal-coloured, slipper-like pumps he wore.

They were both silent until the gong sounded. Lattimer gave her his arm.

As they dined, she watched his face closely, trying not to give too much away. She could no longer hide the truth from herself.

He looked her way, and she blushed furiously at being found out.

He frowned uneasily and became grave.

Afterward, Scarlett retired to the drawing room. She resolved to speak with him in his room where there would be more privacy. She hoped he would understand. It had not become customary for her to go to his room. Her heartbeat hard in her chest at the thought of breaking this custom, and of what she must say to him whilst there.

When the time came, and she made her way to his room, her legs were like lead.

The door opened and Edwards, her husband's valet, stared down at her.

She froze, deliberating how to proceed. She had not thought of the valet. "Edwards, I would like to speak with my husband," she said, calming her voice that threatened to wobble.

"At once, madam," he said, standing aside.

Mr Lattimer stared at her for a long moment. He was in the middle of undressing and his shirt was half unbuttoned. His cufflinks had been removed, and he had rolled up his sleeves to his elbows.

"I'm sorry to disturb you. I must speak to you urgently," she said, keeping a respectable distance.

The half-smile on his lips assured her that she was not unwelcome.

She smiled also. "May I sit down?" She indicated the chair by his bed.

"If you wish," he said.

She was still for a moment trying to choose her words carefully. Her mind went blank whenever she looked at him.

"Hurry and say what you have to say," Frank said, growing restless.

She decided to focus her gaze on a spot below his left shoulder and pulled the portrait of Tom out from the folds of her gown, handing it to him. He turned pale when he saw what she had in her hand. She was relieved to read no anger in his expression.

"Where did you get it?" he asked in a low tone.

She pointed to the drawer in the corner of the room with trepidation.

His eyes widened. "You have searched my room?"

She nodded. "You gave me no choice." She heard her voice shaking now.

"Oh, is that right? Is that some excuse for your behaviour?" His voice rose a few notches.

"No. It hardly excuses your conduct in the matter, either. I have a right to hear the truth," she said.

"It is none of your business," he said.

"It is my business. You tricked me and made me believe the lie you are living."

"Tell me what you've discovered?"

"Who is the boy in the portrait?"

"You can't guess?" he asked.

"I have an inkling. I need to hear the truth from you, though."

He shook his head. "I will not tell you anything until I know how much you have found out."

"I also found these. . ." She handed him both the birth certificate and the will.

Instead of taking them from her, he shook his head. "I recognise them." His face twisted.

It took all the strength she had not to put her arms around him then and stop him from speaking the awful truth. It would have been easy to wish it all away, yet she needed to work out her own feelings in the matter. Before her was a man she had grown to love with all her heart. Not only that, but she also needed to know who he was if their future was to be secured. She had to continue. Averting her eyes, she spoke again, "You're not Frank Lattimer, are you? Not the real one?"

The words hung in the air between them, a stain on the castle walls.

He turned to face the wall. "I am not Frank Lattimer," he repeated hoarsely, his shoulders drooping.

"The real Frank died in the fire. Isn't that, right? An eyewitness told me that three bodies were carried out of that fire," she said, gently.

He pivoted. "An eyewitness?"

"The former gardener. Mr Morrison?"

He frowned. "I don't remember him."

"He lives in the Old Mill near the cottages. I visited him there. He told me his story after much deliberation. I also have another confession to make. . ." she began.

"You astonish me," he said, reverting to his biting sarcasm.

"I have been in the old ballroom," Scarlett said.

"You have, have you? So, I can list snooping as well as stealing as one of your many faults. It seems strange now that I once thought you to be as pure as a diamond. Your name suddenly becomes appropriate. Maybe we are not so ill-suited after all, you and I," he said.

"There is something else. I also listened to some of your conversations with your aunt. I should say, your mother."

Frank sighed. "Ah, then you know everything."

"I've told you as much as I know. I would like to hear your story from the beginning. If you want to tell me," she said.

"Are you interested?"

"Definitely. I must hear the rest. Please," she pleaded.

"Very well. As you will see from the birth certificate my name is Thomas Danforth. I'm the illegitimate son of Violet Ellingham, born Danforth. My aunt was Mrs Lattimer. My cousin, Frank Lattimer, though I never met them," he explained.

My mother became with child after an affair with my uncle's valet, Banks. He was immediately dismissed, and she never saw him again.

Before her condition became apparent, she was sent away to Italy where my uncle's grandfather was brought up before he came here.

When I was born, I was taken to an orphanage there. My mother insisted that I be brought up English and I had a tutor. That is why I have an excellent accent. . ." He broke off to study the carpet.

"So, that is what Mr Serengeti meant," Scarlett said to herself.

Her husband looked up sharply. "Serengeti? What did he tell you?"

"He told me nothing. I went to see him in London today. He only told me he met you in Italy, and then you lost touch," she said, raising her hands.

"I see. Then that is the errand you had to run."

"That's right. But he was very loyal to you," she said.

"Why are you defending him? You told me to get rid of him. Don't you remember?" he asked.

"Because it is true. He was loyal to you. Please continue," she said.

"All right. My mother brought me here in secret from the orphanage after the Lattimer family were killed and then passed me off as her nephew. She would have lost her connection to Closings for good had she not done so, as the estate is entailed away from the female line. So, it would have passed over to some distant relation of her brother-in-law's.

He did say in his will, however, that any male children my mother bore, would inherit the estate after the death of Frank, if Mrs Lattimer had no more children. I didn't count as I was illegitimate. They did not speak of me again. I did meet Serengeti at the orphanage in Italy, and I gave him the job as my secretary when I met up with him again in London before I came here," he said.

"I wondered how Violet could have pulled it off until William Morrison said she told him she kept Frank hidden away because he was badly traumatised after the fire, and that the doctor was attending him. Do none of the servants know?" she asked.

"Not that I'm aware of. Mrs Radcliffe knew Frank best, so she may have guessed the truth," he said.

"I have another question. What was the document you tried to force me to sign?" she asked.

Lattimer became uneasy and paused before replying. "It was connected to your fortune. I wanted our two fortunes to be bound up in one. I could not let you read it because it contained details of my identity. Serengeti is in on the secret. He could keep the books because I trust him implicitly. He saved my life, as it happens. My life was not good in the orphanage, but he helped me through it."

Scarlett looked at him questioningly. "Did you sign the document?"

"You mean forgery? No, it is still waiting to be signed," he said.

"I may see it?" she asked, holding out her hand.

"You may, but I don't think you will be very compliant after hearing the full facts of my inheritance. I have obtained it by false pretences, and if I am found out, you will go down with me," he said.

Scarlett gazed at the floor. He was right. How could the love she felt growing inside her survive such a shock? Such a deception as this? She rose suddenly and threw up her hands. "I must go at once. I can't bear it!"

Frank didn't attempt to bar her from leaving his room. He couldn't deny he had used her sorely, and though he would be repaid severely for the offence by losing her, he couldn't help but deplore the unfairness of the outcome.

ONCE SHE WAS IN HER room, Scarlett frantically threw gowns into a suitcase, lying on the bed. She was wretched. The castle had become her home and she had grown fond of it, and of him. Frank Lattimer, the man she almost refused to marry. It had the makings of a fairy tale ending and now, to face such a setback. Never did she suspect for one moment that the secret looming over the castle would affect her so completely.

She turned to stare out of the window, still clinging to a gown.

"What are you doing?" Naima said, finding her mistress staring absently out of the window, the room in disarray with gowns and shoes scattered everywhere.

"I must get out of here. Will you come with me, Naima?" she asked, pivoting.

"Where will you go?" Naima asked, gathering the scattered gowns. "Buckley House?"

She shook her head. "No, I can't go there. Think of the scandal. We must go abroad. I thought about America. I'm familiar with it on the map. My father taught me about the colonies there and the name of Henson should blend in. We might hide out there to ride out the storm."

"But how will you live?" Naima asked.

"I'll think of something. We might get lucky and find Romone Martin waiting for me. We just have to go," Scarlett said.

Naima stroked her chin.

"What's on your mind?" Scarlett asked, familiar with her maid's expression whenever she was about to come up with an idea.

"Can't you work things out with the master?" Naima asked.

Scarlett lowered her eyes and perched on the bed. "This is an awkward dilemma. When I think there was a time this news would have delighted me. What a tidy excuse to be rid of him. I now find myself wishing it away."

Naima gaped. "Are you telling me you have fallen in love with the master?"

Scarlett blushed.

Naima sat beside her mistress to steady herself, a forbidden action for a maid in her lady's chamber, but these petty rules didn't seem to matter anymore.

"You're full of surprises," Naima said when she had recovered. "When did you become aware of your feelings? If it's not too impertinent to ask...?"

Scarlett spun to face the maid and held her hands. "You may ask whatever you like, especially since I'm no longer going to be the mistress here."

"Then, I may speak plainly?" Naima asked.

She nodded.

"Do not be too hasty in your actions. You may live to regret your decision."

"Oh, Naima! What can I do?" She placed her head in Naima's lap.

The maid stroked her hair. "Go to the master. Talk to him again. Maybe there's a way you can work through this together."

"I can't see how," Scarlett said, lifting her head.

Naima lowered her gaze.

"Sorry. Your advice is always sound, but on this occasion, I really don't believe anything can help," Scarlett said.

"Don't do anything tonight. You should sleep on it. It might be that the light of the morning will clear matters up for you," Naima said.

Scarlett agreed and Naima helped her into bed.

WAKING IN THE MORNING, it came as a surprise to Scarlett to find she'd slept the whole night through. It was the most refreshing sleep she'd had in a long while. Grief must have made her weary.

Naima was asleep in the chair beside her bed with her chin lowered towards her chest. She awoke with a groan when Scarlett touched her hand still resting on the covers.

"I must have dozed off," Naima said, smoothing her clothes and standing to attention.

"Don't trouble yourself, Naima. I appreciate how you have looked after me," Scarlett said faintly, her head on the pillow with her hair spread out.

"If it wasn't for me, you'd be half-way overseas by now," the maid said, gathering Scarlett's clothes from the ground. "Let's get you dressed, and then decide how to proceed." Naima flung open the doors to the wardrobe and chose a suitable morning gown.

After breakfast, Scarlett stole downstairs, dreading a meeting with her husband until she found he had left in the early hours, and he wouldn't be back until late.

She filled the day with activities. A long walk about the grounds, painting in the gardens after lunch. She was glad of the diversion, but she was nonetheless alarmed when Frank wasn't home for dinner, and she wondered if he would spend the night in London.

At length, his carriage was heard, but it wasn't until she had dressed for bed.

Scarlett held out her shaking hands while Naima dressed her. "I'm still at a loss. I must decide soon."

Naima was silent and thoughtful for a while.

With the maid's eyes brightening suddenly, Scarlett started. "You've had an idea!"

"Possibly, but I'm not sure if you will approve, and I can't promise it will make matters right," Naima said.

"I'm listening."

Once she was dressed and Naima had given her instructions, Scarlett stole along the hall, her nerves in jitters as she entered Frank's room once again.

The room was dimly lit, and Frank was lying on his bed, his arms under his head.

Softly, she approached his side and whispered his name.

He shot up, wiping at his brow. "Are you still here?" He thought she was an apparition.

She nodded.

"You can't mean to stay?" he asked.

"Frank. I've been thinking about what you told me of the will."

"What about it?"

"Why is it false? If you had not been born out of wedlock, and had your father been a gentleman, the circumstances of the will would make it legal for you to inherit Frank Lattimer's fortune and estate," she said.

He laughed wildly and shook his head. "You do not understand, my dear. I doubt any lawyer would see it that way. The fact is, I am cut out of the will."

"But no one will find out. What I'm saying is that you have a right to it in principle. I believe in justice for those who are downtrodden in society," she said.

"Do you? Well, clearly not everyone is as generous as you are. I'm aware how much you hate society's rules in general," he said.

"Yes, and I hate it even more now. . ." her voice faded.

He smiled at her. "So, you see? If I'm found out, you will have me, but no fortune. That is a pitiable prospect, indeed. It is a good thing you refused to sign that document. You would be penniless with an illegitimate husband. What would your father say to that?"

"My father? He cares nothing for money. He follows as my mother leads. That's all," she said, her eyes brightening.

"Are you serious?"

"What do you mean?" Her cheeks grew hot when she detected the sarcasm in his tone. "You don't know him as I do."

He breathed deeply. "Oh, Scarlett." He dropped his hands by his sides.

Scarlett's eyes were glued to him.

"I think you'd be surprised. Do you know what he said to me when I asked him for your hand?" he asked.

She remained silent, staring at him with wide-eyed wonder.

"He told me the inheritance was all that mattered to them. You were at their disposal, it seems, dear," he said.

"Did he really say that?" she whispered.

"I wouldn't lie to you." He held his hands out before him.

"Would you not?"

"I love you! I'm afraid you're stuck with me," he said.

She got to her feet, edging closer, hardly aware that she had done so. When she reached his side, she leaned in close and pushed a stray curl back into place on his forehead. "It seems you are stuck with me too," she whispered, before gently kissing him.

CHAPTER TWENTY-SEVEN

The sun had risen over Closings when Scarlett awoke in her husband's room. For a moment she had forgotten the happy outcome and reconciliation of last night until she glanced over at Frank who was sound asleep beside her.

She stole noiselessly from the bed. Once she reached the exit, he stirred and opened his eyes. "Where are you sneaking off to?" he whispered, sitting up. "We need to talk."

"Isn't it all settled?" Scarlett said, her hand on the handle of the door.

"I believe there is more to say. You see, I cannot think about the way I treated you without abhorrence," he said.

Scarlett dropped her hand from the door and sauntered to his side, kneeling at his feet. "I have forgiven you everything. You were in a lonely place. With such a secret hanging over our heads, we could never have found any peace."

"I'm relieved to hear you say so." He bent his head over her and kissed her hair.

Later, she looked out onto the balcony of her own chamber and a fine mist had set in over the east.

When Naima entered with a breakfast tray, she found her mistress wide awake and sat up in her bed with a dreamy smile playing on her lips.

"Naima!" she said, her face becoming radiant.

"You look happy this morning," Naima said suspiciously, pausing by the door, a tray in her hand.

"I am. Thank you, Naima."

"It worked; I see. Are we going to stay at Closings?" Naima asked.

"It did work. It is all settled, and I'm honoured to remain the mistress of Closings. I'm grateful you talked me into it. Frank was very loving, and we will do very well together."

Naima stepped back a few paces. "If you carry on saying such things, I will have no choice but to leave the room at once."

"Right. I'll be sensible again. Might I have my breakfast?" Scarlett asked.

"I would do better not to inquire any further, I think. Enjoy your breakfast." Naima placed the tray of Eggs Benedict, a pot of coffee, and a glass of fresh orange juice on her lap.

"WHAT? YOU'RE TELLING me she went to his room unbidden?" Sarah said upon hearing of the escapade from Mr Latimer's valet in the kitchen.

"Yes, Sarah, I am. I'm not joking," Edwards said.

"Well, I never. They must be reconciled," Sarah said. "I knew she was never conventional that one, though." She shook her head.

"The master was cheerful this morning too. Whistling away he was. He was smiling too," the valet said.

"Now, there's a rare thing," the parlour maid said, giggling.

"I hope you are not speaking out of turn, the pair of you?" Larsson said, entering the kitchen.

Sarah stood to attention alongside Edwards.

"I told the pair of you about idle chit-chat before. Don't you have work to get on with?" Larsson said.

They bowed respectfully and bustled out of the kitchen.

When he was left alone, Larsson fought a strong urge to have his curiosity satisfied about the recent goings-on in the household. A suspicion he'd long held was in danger of coming out in the open. He clenched his hands into fists. He would protect the family name at all costs.

He pondered what the disclosure might mean for the staff.

AFTER BREAKFAST SCARLETT headed downstairs.

Larsson handed her a couple of letters.

She recognised the handwriting of Catherine and her mother. She snatched them off the tray. For a long while, she'd been tapping her fingers to hear from Catherine about her wedding preparations.

"Where did Mr Lattimer say he was going this morning?" she asked Larsson, stopping in the doorway of the parlour.

"I believe he has gone to Mr Serengeti's office in London, ma'am," Larsson said.

She headed for the morning room where a fire had been lit early that morning and had risen to a welcoming glow. She took a seat by the bay window overlooking the orchard in the distance. The gardener, Prichard, was there tending to the plants, and he looked up and waved as he always did at the same time each morning, aware she would be watching. She waved back and then got stuck into her letters. She read Catherine's letter first.

'My dear Scarlett,

It is too long since I saw you last. There is a void in my heart now I don't have you to talk to. I need you now more than ever, for there are such bad tidings to bring to you, my dearest friend. Your mama has persuaded mine to put a stop to my engagement to Captain Jepson, and she is trying to marry me off to Lord Melhorn, of all people. That old bore. Please, Scarlett, come and persuade your mama otherwise, if possible. I require your help.

Your most affectionate friend,

Catherine.'

At the mention of her mother's schemes, Scarlett threw the letter aside. She picked up her mother's letter, staring at it like it contained venom, and ripped open the seal.

'Dearest Scarlett,

I'm afraid that I do not have glad tidings to bring to you, my dear. I will come straight to the point so as not to alarm you. Alas, your father is gravely ill. Doctor Donaldson attends to him, and he informs me he is suffering from acute pneumonia. I must urge your immediate assistance.

Your most affectionate and deeply troubled,

Mama.'

Scarlett sat back in her chair, her brow creased and her thoughts softening. Tears streamed down her cheeks. This was too much to bear. It was difficult not to feel vexed with her mama for her involvement in her friend's distress. But here was her father very ill, and her mama in great distress herself. What should she do? What a difference her mood had undergone since breakfast. She resolved to wait for her husband's return at luncheon.

She pursed her lips when she pulled back the curtains to see that Violet had accompanied her husband in his carriage. A minute later, another carriage pulled up and Mr Serengeti appeared. She rushed out to find them all assembled on the porch as Larsson collected their coats.

Much to her surprise, Violet stepped forward first and stiffly kissed her. Scarlett couldn't tell what had caused this sudden change in her manner, and although distress had made her weary, she played along, answering pleasantly, "Violet. I'm happy to see you."

"And I you, but I must speak with you, my dear. If I may?" Violet indicated the sitting room.

Scarlett turned to her husband, who could only smile at her as he led Mr Serengeti towards his study.

"My son has told me you're fully informed of all the circumstances regarding his birth and of my disgrace," Violet said when they were settled, and Sarah had brought them some tea.

"Yes," Scarlett whispered.

With her head bent, Violet said, "I must apologise for hitting you. I misjudged you." She leaned back as if relieved to let go of the guilt she carried.

Scarlett inclined her head and waited for her to continue.

As Violet took her hand, it felt cold to the touch. "You must understand that I meant you no harm, and though affection is not my strongest quality, I hope you can see that everything I have done was to protect my family's good name."

Lifting her head, Scarlett smiled grimly. She knew her new-found love for Frank would allow her to overcome any barrier, and as the woman next to her was his mother, she saw no alternative than to accept her apology. "I think I can concede to that," Scarlett said.

Violet clung to the sofa. "I must ask you to tell me your motives for finding out the truth? Were they to punish my son?"

"Absolutely not. I love your son, Mrs Ellingham, very much. I wanted to find out the truth because I wanted him to share it. It helps a lot, does it not, to share things?" Scarlett said.

Violet scrutinised her features as she was speaking. The light in Scarlett's eyes expressed the warmth she felt inside, and Violet let out a relieved breath. "I see that you are sincere. I hope we understand each other, Scarlett, and that you will keep the secret of Closings."

"With all my heart. I hope very much that we can be friends," Scarlett said.

A slight warmth crept into Violet's expression that Scarlett had never seen there before. "Indeed, we can, and shall."

Scarlett's embrace was returned by a cold pat on the shoulder.

She was called into her husband's study, where Mr Serengeti informed her that the binding document would be left unsigned until after things were settled as the fortune could not afford to be bound up with Closings at the present time.

They all sat down to lunch.

The visitors did not leave until late in the afternoon and her husband had to rush off back to London to attend to another business matter, arriving back at eight o'clock in the evening, and dining alone.

Scarlett waited in her room to broach the subject with him of going to Buckley House.

"May I come in?" he asked, once he'd joined her there.

She stepped back to let him enter.

He took her gently by the waist and pulled her to him. "I regret I've neglected you today, darling." He leaned forward to kiss her.

She pulled away, and then he noticed the distress in her face.

"What is it?" he asked gently.

"I received this letter today from Mama," she said, handing it to him.

He ambled to the window to read it. When he had finished, he came towards her with a frown on his brow. "You actually think it's as serious as it sounds?"

"I think so. Doctor Donaldson knows what he is about," Scarlett said.

"You want to go to your father after what I told you of him?" Something of his old fierceness returned to his voice as he asked the question.

"Of course, I do! He is still my father," she said, her cheeks burning with indignation thinking of the concession she'd made for his mother. "I would like to give him a chance to explain himself."

"Very well. I will escort you there tomorrow." He turned to leave the room.

"Wait!" She rushed to his side, taking his hand. "Don't go," she whispered.

CHAPTER TWENTY-EIGHT

Buckley House was its usual welcoming self as they pulled up in the carriage.

Naima, who had travelled in the servants' carriage alongside Edwards, could not contain her excitement at being back there again, and she rushed off to the kitchen with the valet to introduce him to the staff.

"Scarlett, my dear," Lavinia Henson said, holding out her arms to her daughter and hugging her tightly.

Scarlett drew back coldly. "It is good to see you, Mama. How is Father?"

"He is resting. You may see him later when he has awoken. Ah, Mr Lattimer too," she said as he appeared from behind Scarlett.

Frank nodded politely.

"Come into the drawing room. Now, I hope you don't mind, but Lady Salisbury is here," Mrs Henson said, leading them in.

Before they had a chance to speak, they were mobbed by Lady Salisbury asking after them and Violet.

Once Scarlett had assured her, they were all well, they settled down for tea and cakes.

Mr Lattimer crossed his legs and drank his tea in silence, listening to the constant chatter of Lady Salisbury with distaste.

Scarlett tried to keep her countenance while she waited for an opportunity to confront her mother about Catherine's letter.

When Mrs Henson finally escorted Lady Salisbury to the door, Scarlett followed and tugged at her mother's sleeve. "I need to speak with you, Mama," she whispered.

Lavinia gave her a knowing look and led her into her private sitting room, leaving Lady Salisbury to make her own way out.

Lavinia hurried on in an endless attempt at justification. "I understand what you're going to say, Scarlett. I had no choice. Catherine cannot marry Captain Jepson. Indeed, she cannot. Her mother had to agree with me. She did not approve of the match either, Scarlett. Surely you know that. I..."

"Mother, please. Spare me this," Scarlett said, losing all patience. "First, it was me you chose to marry off, but you were not satisfied leaving it there, were you? You had to interfere with my best friend."

"Nay, Scarlett, I have only ever sought to act in your best interests. I refuse to apologise for that."

"As it happens, I'm very happy with Frank now. I have grown to love him very dearly, but. . ."

Mrs Henson's eyes grew animated. "There, you see? These matches do not always work out badly."

"That is no excuse, Mama. You had no right to interfere with Catherine's engagement. Please, Mama, she loves Captain Jepson. You could use your influence for good there. Can't you see that?"

Lavinia deliberated for a moment. "All right. I will speak to Mrs Kettering tomorrow."

"Thank you, Mama," Scarlett said with a sigh.

They stepped out of the hall in time to see Romone Martin escorted through the door.

"Romone! How good to see you." Scarlett rushed to his side.

"My dear Scarlett. How is your father?" he asked, concern creasing the corners of his eyes.

"He must not be disturbed at present," Lavinia said.

"Ah, I see," Romone said.

"Come into the drawing room, please," Scarlett said, leading him by the sleeve.

Scarlett felt uneasy as she recalled the last meeting between her husband and her friend. "My husband has accompanied me," she whispered. "Be kind to him."

"As far as I can recall it was not I who was unkind," Romone muttered as the door swung open.

Mr Lattimer, who had moved to the fireplace, noticed the exchange with raised eyebrows.

"It is Mr Martin, dear. He has come to see Father," Scarlett said, kissing Frank on the cheek.

"Ah," Frank said with a slight nod.

"Mr Lattimer," Romone said, nodding too. He wouldn't extend his hand.

Dinner was an awkward affair as Mrs Henson had invited Romone to stay until Mr Henson felt ready to receive visitors. As the evening wore on, their guest decided he had to take his leave with a promise to Mrs Henson to call again soon. Scarlett accompanied him to the door, much to Lattimer's consternation.

"Now that we are alone, I have a piece of news to share with you, which I think will please you," Romone said.

"You have met someone," she said warmly, touching his arm.

"Yes. Her name is Delphine. She is a delightful French girl. You were right, there was someone. I had only to wait."

"I am delighted for you both. I hope very much to be able to meet her soon. In the meantime, you must write to me and fill me in with all the details about her," she said.

As she prepared for bed in her old room, Scarlett felt some anguish at the meeting with her father being postponed until tomorrow. She stared at her reflection in the familiar mirror.

Lattimer came in softly, placing his hands on her shoulders. "Have you recovered, my love?" he asked, noticing her creased brow.

"I wish I could have spoken to my father today. It is strange to be back in this room, and with you," she said, leaning her head back on his chest.

"What about Martin? You seemed familiar with him this evening. I'm sorry I must ask..." He broke off, fighting a frown.

She spun on the chair. "I am familiar with him because he is like a brother to me. I have come to realise that. You have nothing to fear, and I have reason to believe that he is to be very soon engaged," she said with a fixed gaze.

"Is that so?" Frank asked.

"I'm so happy for him!" Scarlett said.

"Did you manage to bring your mother round about Miss Kettering?" he asked with a smile.

"I have got her cooperation. I think we can allow her more credit than we thought possible," Scarlett said.

MR HENSON RECEIVED Scarlett in his dressing room on the following afternoon. She put her head in at the door cautiously and found him propped up in his bed in the dimmed light.

"Come here, my child," he said hoarsely, followed by a coughing fit.

"Father," she said, her lips drooping.

"It has passed for now. Sit down here," he said, pointing to the chair beside his bed.

She complied, opening her mouth to speak.

He signed for her to be silent. "I have wronged you greatly. . ."

"Father, no. . .!"

"Hush, my love. I have wronged you. I told Mr Lattimer that I cared only for the inheritance and influence you would have on becoming his wife. That, though, is not true. It has vexed and sorely troubled me ever since," Mr Henson said, gasping for air.

"Father. Please don't distress yourself. It has turned out to be a blessing in disguise. My maid, Naima, is always telling me how circumstances always turn out right in the end if we're patient and give them a chance to work. I love my husband very dearly. I'm grateful you brought him into my life. I would never have known him otherwise," Scarlett said.

Mr Henson wept, bringing on another coughing fit.

Once the fit had passed, she reached out and embraced him. "Would you like to speak with Frank?"

"I would like that."

"I will call him," she said, getting to her feet. As she stood up, the room spun around as a light-headedness overtook her.

The next sensation she knew was lying on her bed where Frank had carried her. Doctor Donaldson stood over her.

Frank paced the room, running his fingers through his hair. "Are you all right? Scarlett," he asked, aware she was awake. He paused by the bed, bringing her hand up to his lips.

"I think so," she whispered. "What happened?"

"You have fainted, Mrs Lattimer. But all seems well. I must examine you, if Mr Lattimer would allow me?" the doctor said, glancing at Frank.

"I will just be outside," Frank said, hesitating.

Later, Doctor Donaldson came out of Scarlett's room and placed a hand on Frank's shoulder. His expression was serious.

"What is it, Doctor?" Frank asked, fear in his eyes.

"It is nothing that nine months will not cure, sir. Congratulations! You're going to be a father," the doctor said.

Mr Lattimer staggered backward.

Doctor Donaldson held out his hand. "You must believe it, sir."

Frank shook his hand and rushed into the room to be at Scarlett's bedside, hugging her as she sat up to welcome him.

She smiled up at him. "Are you pleased, Frank?"

"I could not be more so," he said.

Frank then uttered the words he would repeat often. "I could not have asked for anything more. I never would have imagined things could end so well in my life after such a wretched beginning. Thank you for making it possible."

CHAPTER TWENTY-NINE

"We can celebrate properly now we are home," Frank said, relieved they finally had a moment to themselves without the influence of relatives hanging over them.

"We certainly can. It is a fine evening for it," Scarlett replied, looking out on the tranquil scene of trees surrounding them. The gold and orange tones of the autumnal leaves scattered on the lawn and danced on the lake in the distance.

They dined on the terrace that night.

Scarlett had to agree it was about time they began their life together now that the air was clear between them. This is what they were celebrating as well as their exciting news from the doctor. "I cannot wait to watch our children grow up here," she said, patting her belly.

Frank smiled; the strain completely vanished from his face. "What a marvelous place for such a prospect."

She nodded eagerly. "And in the wintertime, I can see us sitting by a firelight, frost upon the windows, and our children at our feet."

With this vision before her eyes, the meal in front of them was a delight, having picked at her food like a bird since they had repaired to the castle.

The soup starter tasted saltier, the flesh of the sea bass fell off the bones and melted on her tongue. The Apple Charlotte dessert tasted sweeter.

Together they watched the sun setting above the castle walls and the scene was full of hope.

WHEN MRS RADCLIFFE hovered by the entrance to the morning room, a question quivered on her lips. Her hesitancy made her more frightening, somehow.

"Did you want me?" Scarlett asked. Her fingers paused in the middle of writing a letter.

"We need to get a few matters cleared up, madam," the housekeeper said, entering collectedly.

Scarlett dropped the quill and faced her. "You'd best tell me at once." She rubbed her face. How many more revelations could she stand that day?

Reaching the fireplace, Mrs Radcliffe began to stoke the dying embers. She felt an overwhelming need to work while in the presence of her mistress. "Prepare yourself."

"I'm willing to hear what you have to say," Scarlett said, her hands nestled in her lap.

The housekeeper reached inside the folds of her ebony gown, drawing out an envelope. From a distance, she handed it to Scarlett, continuing to stare at the glowing coals until her mistress was through with reading the words she'd penned almost thirty years before.

Stratton House, 1803

'My dear niece,

I'm finding the work here difficult given the loss of my mistress. I'd formed a strong bond with her that I cannot find with anyone else. It was tricky to leave Closings after all those pleasant years spent in the Lattimer's employment. I'm eagerly anticipating the day when their son Frank will take on the running of the estate. I have the word of Violet Ellingham that I will be considered first to resume my work as the housekeeper as soon as that happy day is upon us.

Speaking of Frank Lattimer, however, I must mention an unusual circumstance that happened at the park today. I was taking the morning air when I saw Violet with the boy. I got a shock, for he was not the way I remembered him at all. What happened to his beautiful yellow hair? Could the short gap of not seeing him, my dear Betsey, have really changed him that much? He has such a sickly, pale constitution too. . .'

The letter was cut short, and Scarlett glanced curiously at Mrs Radcliffe, who met her gaze.

"Yes, I had a revelation right there as I spelt out those words. As I saw how the letter would be construed, I wanted it destroyed. But even burning it would have been too risky. A servant might have seen the remains of it," Mrs Radcliffe said.

"You've kept it safe for all these years?" Scarlett asked.

"I thought I'd misplaced it with some other important documents when Redwood stayed here. What a disaster that would have been. . .!" She dropped the poker and nursed her head. "Yet, not to worry. I found it stuck to the floor of the safe. I've kept it on my person ever since," the housekeeper added.

With a deep breath, Scarlett passed her back the letter.

Snatching it from her hands, Mrs Radcliffe tucked it away.

They remained silent for a long while.

"I'm not sure why, but I get a sense of relief from your letter," Scarlett said, breaking the silence. "I do not know why you remained loyal to Frank after this. . ."

"That's easy, madam. I wished to protect my Isabella. Although she was not always content here, it was her beloved Closings. I mean to keep these walls, and with them her name, free of reproach," the housekeeper said.

Scarlett held a hand above her heart. "Your concern is deeply appreciated."

"The moment I sensed you could be trusted, I wanted you to find out Frank's identity. That's the only way any discord between you and. . . the master, could ever be reconciled," Mrs Radcliffe said.

Scarlett got to her feet. "You must burn that letter immediately."

Mrs Radcliffe obeyed. They guarded the fireplace until they saw the last words turn to ash.

CHAPTER THIRTY

Four Years later

The same sun would still shine, and the sky would glisten above Closings Castle, only now it was a happy home and the Lattimer's children played around them.

The dark cloud had lifted from the castle and with it, Parsons Running. It was as if the smoke from the fire had finally dispersed, and the villagers could breathe again. The result was that the village was once again the friendly place it had always been renowned for.

Frank Lattimer had become a more agreeable master now that his true generosity was able to shine through, with Scarlett by his side.

While it was true her father was gone, Scarlett was content in the knowledge that they had got their feelings out in the open, and that she had repaired the troubled relationship with her mother, not least because she had brought Frank and her together. Yet, it couldn't be said of Lavinia that she had learnt her lesson. On the contrary, she was a more determined matchmaker than ever.

The ball was organised to a more satisfactory level with Violet Ellingham being persuaded to step back and allow Scarlett to govern as the mistress. Her cordiality might be trickier to win over, but Scarlett was working on her, and she hoped the simplicity of their children's nature would soften her in time.

Her faithful maid, Naima, was always by her side. As a mother, Scarlett found comfort in leaving her two children to her charge. She had no doubt she would pass on to them some of her Irish wisdom and charm.

Lights glistened from the chandeliers in the ballroom. Guests danced into the early hours of the morning.

Even Julian Slater had got his invitation sealed to visit them as often as he wanted. He simply doted on the couple and their children. "You were right, old chum," he told Frank after his debut visit to Closings. "It is a special place, and you were right to keep it to yourself."

Frank insisted he was not, and they left the debate there until they cared to pick it up again.

After the ball, and in the first light of the morning, a couple appeared amongst the floral hedgerows on horseback. Patting the head of the elegant white stallion, Scarlett relaxed at the sight of those far away hills.

"I'll race you," Frank said, turning to his wife.

"Yes. But my dear, Mr Lattimer. I'll win. I always do," she replied.

He grinned. "There's always a first time." He raced down the hill and Scarlett followed. They galloped side by side into the sunset.

If you enjoyed *The Secret of Closings,* you'll love Laura Walker's, *The Case of the Disappearing Earl*

It all started when Lord Sandford disappeared from the abbey . . .

1911: Orphan Marie Wilder works at Sandford Abbey as a Lady's maid to the Earl of Sandford's daughter, Lady Annabelle Croydon. When the earl mysteriously disappears after a dinner, with guests including the famous actress, Blanche Villiers, Marie, who loves the detective stories of Arthur Conan Doyle, is curious and begins investigating. After a rocky start, she eventually wins the respect of the DCI in charge of the case, Jonathan Bailey. But is love waiting in the wings?

Out soon in paperback

An extract follows here . . .

The Case of the Disappearing Earl

Marie Wilder's Diary, 1925

No one dared to speak their mind on the night Lord Sandford disappeared. As if saying their thoughts aloud would somehow spell out the terrible secret that remained hidden with his absence. It was a specifically cold winter that year, but I remember the abbey was lively, full of guests and good cheer, at least outwardly, when you consider the night before the family were happily immersed in the abbey ballroom for the Sandford Ball. Watching from the side-lines, the other servants and I revelled in the bright lights of the chandeliers illuminating the synchronised couples twirling around the dancefloor in their finery. The gentlemen's suit jackets spread out behind them, gathering speed. Ladies silk and lace gowns trailed on the ground like spinning tops. I watched my lady's face light up as she danced, admiring my handiwork on the rose gold dress with a square neckline, and fine gauze sleeves draped at her elbows. It was the most enjoyment I'd seen my lady have in a long while.

How quickly the shadows can creep up on us.

It was also a very special time for me in more ways than one. I came alive again and found a home, a family.

There was an ancient tomb in the abbey grounds. You were only aware of its existence if you sought it out. The moon spotlighting the estate was bright. On the ground floor, a window flapped against the wall in the breeze, blowing the curtains wide. Inside, the room was filled with an empty desolation of want, of a need that would never be realised; however fervently it was sought-after. As the lonely embers burned out in the grate, that need would never return to claim what it rightfully owned.

SANDFORD, 1911

Sandford Abbey was the stately home of the century. A sprawling Jacobean manor that could be seen poking from the tops of the trees in the town of Sandford. When people drew up outside the entrance after journeying through miles of lush greenery, they were often overwhelmed by the sense of art in the parapets and intricate stonework that made up its walls.

A bunch of keys jingled on the chatelaine chain at the waist of Mrs Eileen Norris as she made the long walk down the cold, stone corridor from the Sandford Abbey drawing room to the servant's quarters. She had served as Head Housekeeper at the abbey for nearly twenty years and now, with a few grey hairs sprung up in her raven bun, she knew the house like it was her own. She pushed open the heavy, wooden door to the housekeeper's sitting room, her grease black dress scrunching, and looked inside.

A Lady's maid of six and twenty, Miss Marie Wilder, was seated in the room's corner at the desk, her nose nestled in a book. As it was evening, she had loosened her auburn hair from the high bun she always wore whilst working, and it draped down her back, reaching to her waist. Her feet were resting on a footstool under the desk. The book was placed over the folds of the corselet skirt she wore with a blouse tucked into the high waistband.

"What? You reading again? Miss Marie. Can't be good for your eyesight," Mrs Norris said, after watching her for a while.

Marie looked up, her cocoa eyes speckled with amber, startled. Hers was a beauty that was not immediately apparent and could be passed over for plainness on first appearances. It was strengthened by her intelligence and in her manner of addressing a person. Many found she had boundless charm and were thus drawn to her. "Sorry, what was that? Mrs Norris," Marie said.

"Not good for your hearing either, I see. All this book reading. What is it you're reading this time?" Mrs Norris asked.

"Oh, it's the latest Arthur Conan Doyle novel. It's superb!"

Eileen rolled her eyes. "Another detective story. You'll be getting fanciful ideas in your head filling it with all that nonsense."

"Sherlock Holmes is a very great detective. I've often wanted to meet a real-life detective, especially one like Mr Holmes," Marie said.

Mrs Norris raised a cleft chin. "I think you'll find the police are not so enchanting in real life."

"I can't tell you what they're like," Marie said, her mouth drooping. The truth was, Mr Holmes had become like a friend to her; she'd never had many. That's where the comfort of a good book came from.

"Well, I don't think you'll be finding out. At least I hope not."

"You never can tell," Marie said.

"I'm not trying to put a stop to your reading, only you be careful." She stared at the ceiling as she added, "I recall when I was a housemaid in my old place. The scullery maid, Rosemary something or other... she got the sack through too much daydreaming. She lacked motivation."

"I'm sure that won't happen. A small taste of daydreaming can spur us on in this job," Marie said.

"In a way... Just don't let it affect your work, Child."

"I won't, Mrs Norris."

"Well, then... I was just in the drawing room, Lady Annabelle was asking for you," Mrs Norris said.

Marie slammed the book shut, placing it in the deep pocket of her skirt.

"She says she'll see you in her chamber," Mrs Norris said.

Marie retraced Mrs Norris' steps towards the drawing room, shivering with the cold from the draughty passages. She angled the tasselled shawl tighter around her shoulders and climbed the steps.

She crossed the divide between servants and aristocracy.

Upon reaching the drawing room, she saw the doors were open slightly, and she stole across the gap in the centre, so she could avoid detection from Lady Sophia Sandford, the earl's new wife of two years, who was twenty years his junior. She usually sat alone in the evenings, which is why Marie was startled to hear voices within. She paused on the other side of the gap to listen.

It was the voice of a gentleman she did not recognise. It wasn't Lord Sandford's grouchy old voice, but that of a much younger man, nearer to Lady Sandford's age.

"How is the old man?" he said.

"Clifton? Oh, you know, same as ever," Lady Sandford said in her sing-song voice.

"How many other old men are there in your life?" he asked.

Lady Sandford laughed.

There was a chink of a glass and Marie guessed he was pouring himself a drink.

"Darling, how are you fixed for escorting me to Paris when I get my inheritance?" Lady Sandford asked after a short pause.

The man gave a wicked laugh. "Well, you don't stand to inherit this place, and one must live somewhere."

"Yes, one must, mustn't one," Lady Sandford said.

Marie could sense the familiar vibe of two lovers.

"I say, how much of a fortune do you inherit?" he asked.

"I cannot say exactly," she replied.

"You mean you're being torturingly tight-lipped about it," he said.

"That has rather a nice ring to it. You always have a way with words," Lady Sandford said.

"Don't I? I'm exceedingly proud of myself," he said. "I suppose Paris is as good as anywhere."

"You're hard to please, you know that? Many people would jump at a chance to go to the most romantic city in the world," she said.

"Let's not get ahead of ourselves. Let us not forget Rome," he said.

"Rome it is, then."

"I have a cousin in Rome too. He will set us up with somewhere to live," he said.

Marie jumped as she recognised the butler's heavy footsteps echoing against the wall. She dashed from the scene, racing up the burgundy carpet on the grand staircase. When she reached Lady Annabelle's bedroom, she tapped lightly on the door.

Lady Annabelle's muffled voice invited her inside.

Stealthily, she entered the jade green room with silk, scarlet bed sheets. She stood to attention before Her Ladyship with her clasped hands resting in front of her.

Lady Annabelle, dressed in a sheer ivory dressing gown with a lace edge over a long, embroidered nightgown, was seated at the walnut dressing table, still facing the mirror. Marie could see her anguished face looking back at her. Her ivory skin was paler still in the dull light. To see the two young women together, one would think they were twins as they were almost identical with their long, auburn hair, until one looked closely at Lady Annabelle's complexion, which was much paler than Marie's tanned one, and her eyes were of a hazel hue.

Lady Annabelle Croydon turned around at last but stayed seated. Marie looked her sympathy for the wretched girl, having the knowledge of what she had been through these past weeks that showed in the deep recesses of her skin.

Seeing Annabelle in such a state of distress made Marie's mind wander to the personal tragedy that shook her own life to the crux. The day the shopkeeper from Selby high street, Mr Wickes, her neighbour at the time, broke the news of her parent's accident, was still vivid in her mind. She was six years old when it happened, quickly becoming a broken shell of the happy child she used to be. The police had told Mr Wickes while she was at school, and he found the gentlest possible way to break it to her even though his eyes showed how much he was averted to the task. Now, it was as if her parents, and the life she lived then, had never existed at all.

She recalled with a renewed spirit of the day she started work at the abbey as a housemaid after finishing her schooling at Sandford Orphanage. She had grown as close to Her Ladyship as it was possible for a servant to be to a member of the Sandford family during her time there, and especially as Annabelle had been so kind about her parents.

"Ah, Wilder. Just the woman. I seem to have lost a broach," Annabelle said.

"Oh? How strange," Marie said, frowning.

"I wouldn't bother, only it's the one my mother left me on her death bed," Annabelle said, shuffling the contents of her jewellery box around.

Marie pictured the oval, gold trimmed broach containing a cameo of the late Lady Sandford. "It is very important to you, my lady," she said.

"Indeed, and rather expensive."

"I haven't seen it since last evening when you wore it for the ball," Marie said.

"Quite."

Marie hurried over and checked the contents for herself.

"I'll mention it to Dawson," Marie said, after assuring herself it wasn't in the room.

"Yes, I'm sure there's a perfectly innocent explanation."

Marie nodded, heading for the door.

Annabelle's lips parted in the mirror, her face contorting. "Oh, Wilder. Do you ever feel like a caged bird? Desperate to be freed?" she said, swiping a hand across her forehead.

"I don't know, my lady. I haven't really thought about it," Marie said, edging back into the room.

"But surely you do. You're a servant. Wouldn't you like to be your own person?" she asked, eyeing her closely.

Marie gave her a tight smile.

"Oh, come on, Wilder. You can tell me. I won't throw you over or anything. After... well... perhaps it is best not to speak the words, but you know me well enough to know, I shan't breathe a word of anything you tell me," Annabelle said.

"I'm aware of that, my lady. It is just that I'm not sure what it is like to be free."

"No, I suppose not, as you were brought up in that frightful orphanage." Annabelle shuddered. Marie was aware of the reason.

"There's often a hidden solution, my lady," Marie said, her voice softening. "We just need to search harder sometimes to find it." She wasn't certain there was such a solution on this occasion.

Annabelle laughed. It was a despairing laugh that Marie found heart-breaking. She stood up and moved towards Marie until her lips were close enough to her ear. "Did you?" she whispered, fear in her eyes, as though speaking the secret she bore aloud would somehow make it more reproachful.

Marie nodded. "It is done."

Relief flooded Annabelle's face. "Is all well?"

"Yes, my lady."

"Then I may sleep at least a tiny bit easier tonight," she said, moving towards her bed. She emphasised the word, "tiny' with her fingers. She threw off her robe and nestled under the duvet. "Goodnight, Wilder."

"Goodnight, my lady."

Marie lifted the heel of her shoe, stretching the arched strap along the ankle, and crept on her toes along the same route that had taken her there, until she reached her own room, where, with a heavy sigh, she undressed and climbed into bed, taking up her book again. She felt an overwhelming pity in her heart for Lady Annabelle and her plight. She was probably the nearest to a friend she'd ever had. Even though *she* was the orphan and the other brought up high, there was almost an equalising in fellow feeling and a reverse role tonight.

About the Author

Laura Walker grew up in the Derbyshire Dales and she now lives with her husband in Staffordshire. She has been writing since childhood and specialises in regency romance and mystery novels.

Read more at friendlyebooks4u.wixsite.com/laurawalker-1.

Ingram Content Group UK Ltd.
Milton Keynes UK
UKHW011838040423
419625UK00004B/352